WHEN DARKNESS FALLS

BOOK 1

ANA GUTIERREZ

When Darkness Falls

Copyright © 2025. Ana Gutierrez

Book Design by Transcendent Publishing

ISBN: 979-8-9922207-7-3

This book is a work of fiction. Names, characters, and incidents are a product of the author's imagination or used fictitiously. Any resemblance to persons, living or dead, is entirely coincidental.

Printed in the United States of America.

CONTENT ADVISORY

This book contains themes of self-harm and
mental health challenges,
which may be disturbing to some readers.
Reader discretion is advised.

In the beginning God created the heaven and the earth.

*And the earth was without form, and void; and darkness was
upon the face of the deep. And the Spirit of God moved upon
the face of the waters.*
And God said, Let there be light: and there was light.
*And God saw the light, that it was good: and God divided the
light from the darkness.*
*And God called the light Day, and the darkness he called Night.
And the evening and the morning were the first day.*
Genesis 1:1-5 (King James Version)

CHAPTER 1

Tick-tock, tick-tock.

The room falls eerily silent, the doctor's words echoing like distant whispers.

Ba-bump, ba-bump, ba-bump.

My heart pounds against my chest so fiercely that it drowns out the world around me. The news strikes me like a sudden gust of wind, ripping through the very fabric of my existence, leaving me gasping for air.

Seated in this sterile, suffocating hospital room, the only sound reaching my ears is the monotonous ticking of the clock on the wall. I strain to comprehend the doctor's words, my gaze fixated on his mouth, desperately attempting to decipher the incomprehensible. I can see his lips moving, yet all I hear is the ringing in my ears and the thumping of my heart.

"Mrs. Lopez?"

I clasp my trembling hands together, seeking solace in the tangible sensation, grounding myself in the present.

"Is there anyone you'd like us to contact for you?"

I shake my head, words caught in my throat.

"Once again, I'm sorry for your loss."

With those words, the doctor turns and leaves. The weight of his message settles in my chest and it's debilitating. And in that solitary moment, immersed in silence, my emotions become my only company. Fumbling, I reach into my purse and dial my brother's number.

"Hello?"

Words elude me, refusing to form or find their voice.

"Isabella? Hello? I swear, Isabella, I don't have time for your ..." my brother demands.

"He's gone ..." I manage to utter.

"Who's gone?"

"He's gone!" I say.

As the words escape my lips, a wave of sorrow crashes against the shores of my soul, swallowing me whole. The dam holding back my tears finally gives way. Tears stream down my face, mingling with the salty taste of grief that fills my mouth. I gasp for air, yearning for someone to rescue me from the suffocating weight of my emotions.

It has been an agonizing week since I got that fateful phone call about Julian's accident. Stepping into the hospital, I had no idea my life was about to change forever. Now, I'm standing in my dimly lit room, alone, drowning in a sea of grief that feels endless, like it might pull me under at any moment. Today is the day I have to say goodbye to Julian, and just the thought of it makes my throat tighten, a lump forming that I can barely swallow past.

I take deep breaths, trying to steady myself, but the tears are relentless, swelling up despite my efforts to hold them back. In this moment, I feel utterly alone, trapped in the grip of my sorrow, yearning for someone—anyone— to pull me back from the brink of despair.

Before I can collect myself, a gentle knock echoes through the room, startling my fragile composure. "Come in," I call out, my voice a mere whisper.

The door creaks open, revealing Manny's concerned face. He enters quietly, closing the door behind him as if stepping into a sacred sanctuary of shared sorrow.

"You ready to go?" he asks, his voice filled with empathy.

I shake my head, feeling the weight of the impending farewell press upon me. "No, but do I really have a choice?"

I feel Manny's hesitation, his struggle to find the perfect words to ease my pain. But before he can even try, I move towards him, seeking refuge in his presence. I wrap my arms around his waist, burying my face against his chest.

In that moment, everything seems to melt away— the grief, the uncertainty, the weight of the world on my shoulders. I feel his tense muscles slowly relax, his arms wrapping around me in a comforting embrace. It's as if, for just a moment, the world stops spinning and all that matters is the warmth of his arms around me, the steady rhythm of his heartbeat against my cheek.

Manny was always the strong, silent type. He carried the weight of the world on his shoulders, stepping up as both big brother and stand-in parent for Sara and me after our parents passed when we were teens. He wasn't big on showing his feelings, but his actions always spoke louder than words.

He made so many sacrifices for us, like taking that tough job that kept him away from home most of the time. We barely saw him, but his hard work paved the way for us to get through college.

When I called him that life-altering night, I knew I'd rattled him. Sure, it would've been easier to reach out to Sara, who lived just a few miles away. But what I really needed in that moment was my big brother's reassurance. I wanted to hear him say everything would be okay. But the words got stuck in my throat, drowned out by a flood of emotions.

In the end, it was Sara who rushed to the hospital to pick me up, while Manny scrambled to catch a flight home from across the country. It was a reminder that even when words fail us, family is always there to pick up the pieces.

When Sara finally arrived at the hospital, I was a wreck. Tears streamed down my face as she embraced me, her own sobs echoing mine. She tried everything to ease my pain, even pleading with the doctors to prescribe sleeping pills. But they refused, deeming it unnecessary.

Instead, we turned to our Tia Sofía, one of my dad's sisters, who came through with pills from her son, a doctor in Mexico. Those little pills became my lifeline, offering a brief escape from the overwhelming grief that nearly consumed me.

At night, the pills offered solace, guiding me through the darkness and shielding me from the intensity of my sorrow. But with each new day, reality crashes back in, the weight of my loss hitting me all over again.

Stepping outside, I am greeted by a gloomy sky, a fitting backdrop for the occasion. The ride to the church is a blur, and before I know it, I stand facing the towering crucifix behind the altar with Julian's casket placed before it. To my right, my mother-in-law's sobs fill the air. I haven't spent much time with Julian's family, and I can't shake the feeling that they somehow blame me for his death. Especially his mother—who never really approved of me.

As I stand there, my gaze fixed on the casket that holds the lifeless body of my beloved Julian, I feel the heaviness of eyes upon me, whispers lingering in the heavy silence.

In the corner of my eye, a familiar face emerges. Sara stands beside me, her presence a ray of light in the darkness, offering comfort amidst the grief. Her hand finds mine, intertwining our fingers, giving me the strength I need. With Sara by my side, I make my way to our seats, opposite of my disapproving mother-in-law.

As the priest begins the mass, I feel like I am drifting in a fog. The cemetery procession becomes a blur. Faces of people merge together in a haze. Amidst it all, the only constants are Sara and Manny. I know my husband's family is also grieving, but I am consumed by my own pain, unable to shoulder the weight of theirs. They already hold a dislike for me, and no amount of politeness or rudeness on this day will change that perception.

As the minutes pass, the sky shifts from a somber gray to a deepening darkness. I wrap my arms around myself as I observe the mourners slowly trickling away from the cemetery. It takes the combined efforts of my husband's siblings and mine to persuade my mother-in-law to leave, giving me time alone with Julian.

With a heavy heart, I approach the edge of the burial plot, gazing down at the wooden casket. It's a scene that feels all too familiar, reminiscent of the sorrowful farewells I had bid to my own parents. The memory weighs heavily on me as I stand there, the echoes of past grief mingling with the present.

Rain begins to fall, softly at first, then steadily increasing in intensity. I remain rooted to the spot, not wanting to say goodbye. Closing my eyes, I allow the tears to flow freely down my cheeks. Suddenly, I feel a hand on my shoulder, startling me. I open my eyes to find Manny standing beside me, holding an umbrella. Sadness fills his eyes as he looks at me.

"Isabella, it's time to go home," he says gently, holding the umbrella over me, shielding me from the storm.

I stubbornly shake my head. "I'm not ready," I whisper, my voice choked with emotion.

Manny drapes his arm around my shoulders, offering silent support.

"I understand," he says softly, "but you have Sara and me. You don't have to do this alone."

The last time I saw Manny express this much emotion was when our parents passed away. His reassurance offers a glimmer of hope within me, reminding me that even in the darkest of times, there are people who care, people who will stand by me until I find my way back to the light.

"Come on, let's get you home," Manny says gently, pulling me out of my thoughts.

I hesitate and nod reluctantly. My gaze lingers on the casket below before I wipe away my tears.

As Manny leads me toward the car, I glance over my shoulder one last time. The rain intensifies, obscuring my vision, but I can still make out the grave in the distance. My hand brushes the edge of the umbrella, and for a brief moment, I step out from under its shelter, letting the rain drench me. It feels almost purifying, as if the storm is grieving alongside me, washing away the fragments of the life I once knew.

I turn back to Manny who opens the car door for me. I step inside, leaving the cemetery—and Julian—behind. But as the car pulls away, I realize that a part of me is also in that grave with Julian.

The rain blurs the world around me, and I close my eyes. I don't know what lies ahead or how I'll face the days to come. All I know is that I never imagined becoming a widow at twenty-seven. It's not a situation you prepare for. But then again, life has a way of surprising you when you least expect it.

CHAPTER 2

"Ugh, not that one! Take another!" I groan, crinkling my nose at the picture on the screen.

"You look beautiful," Julian insists, his hand steady on the camera, a soft smile pulling at his lips.

"You only say that because I'm your wife," I tease, swatting playfully at his arm.

He chuckles, that warm familiar sound, wrapping around me like a favorite blanket. It's the kind of laugh that makes everything lighter, easier—like nothing could ever go wrong. The distant hum of voices and the clinking of glasses fade away, leaving just us in this perfect, sunlit bubble.

"Julian?"

But then, reality slams into me. The softness of his laughter evaporates, the sharp edge of reality slicing through the warmth of the moment. My eyes snap open, and the familiar burden settles over my chest, as if the very air is too thick to breathe.

He's gone.

Every morning, it's the same cruel trick. I wake up with the echo of his voice and laughter in my ears, only to have it ripped away the moment I open my eyes. The loss floods in all over again, sharp and relentless, like the tide dragging me under.

I sit up in bed, gripping the edge of the blanket like it's the only thing that can keep me steady. I keep replaying memories of our lives. I don't want to forget the sound of his laugh, the way his hand fit perfectly around me, and all the plans we had for the future together. I cling to those memories desperately, afraid that if I let go, they'll slip away from me forever, but I can feel them fading, little by little, like sand slipping through my fingers.

It's been three weeks since Julian's funeral, and the world feels hollow, as if it's been drained of all its color and sound. I feel like I'm standing on the edge of an abyss, staring at an empty future.

A faint knock pulls me out of the haze.

"Elle? You awake?" Sara's voice filters through the closed door, soft but insistent.

I swallow hard, forcing myself to sit up, wiping at my face even though there are no tears. "Yeah. Come in."

The door creaks open, and Sara steps inside. She moved in after Julian died—said the house was too big for me to handle alone. Manny, too, packed up his life and moved closer. It was strange at first, all of us back together under one roof like we were kids again.

Sara sits on the end of my bed, her eyes scanning me like she's trying to measure how fragile I am today. "How'd you sleep?"

I shrug, pulling the blanket to my chin. "Not great. Kept waking up."

"Want me to ask Tia Sofía about those sleeping pills? They helped last time." She says it so casually, as if offering a cup of coffee. But there's something in her eyes, a flicker of concern she's trying to hide.

I hesitate, my fingers playing with the edge of the blanket. The pills make sure I don't keep waking up throughout the night, but it also means I'll be unable to dream and I want to see Julian, even if it's in my dreams. It's the only place where he still exists, where he's still mine.

But maybe…maybe not dreaming at all will also give me a break from my grief. Which I desperately want. I don't want to feel this pain. I don't want to keep waking up to a world where there is no Julian.

The thought twists in my chest, painful and tempting all at once. I swallow hard. "Maybe," I finally say.

Sara reaches out and squeezes my hand, her grip firm. "Take a shower. It's been two days. Then come down—I made chilaquiles."

I nod, even though the thought of getting out of bed feels impossible. But Sara's eyes linger, and I know she won't leave until I at least pretend to try.

"Alright," I mutter, dragging myself out from under the covers as she heads for the door.

The water hits me with a dull thud, warm droplets sliding down my skin. I close my eyes, standing under the stream until the heat seeps into my bones. But no matter how long I stand there, it doesn't wash away the weight pressing down on me.

The house feels like a cavern, every corner too big, too empty. Ever since Julian's funeral, I've barely stepped outside. I keep telling myself I'll get better, that this cloud will lift. But so far, nothing. The only time I've left the house was to visit his parents. I'd thought maybe seeing them would help, that we could lean on each other. But I was wrong.

I had barely made it through the front door before Julian's mother confronted me. Her eyes, sharp with grief and anger, fixed on me as she spoke, her voice rising, brittle and raw.

"Si no te hubiera conocido—si se hubiera alejado de ti—él todavía estaría aquí. Es tu culpa."

Her words pierced through the air, heavy and unforgiving. *Tu culpa.* Your fault. The way she spat the words, full of anger and blame, cut deeper than any knife. It wasn't just an accusation, it felt more like she was giving her verdict, placing everything that had gone wrong *on me.* In her eyes, I wasn't just responsible—I was guilty.

The worst part is that no one else said anything. His father sat quietly, his gaze cast down, while his siblings avoided my eyes. They all just let her accusations hang there, unanswered, as if agreeing with her in silence.

I stood there frozen, every word sinking deeper until I couldn't stand it anymore. I left their house, choking on the weight of their unspoken judgment.

Since then, I haven't gone back.

I rest my forehead against the shower tiles, gasping as the sobs rise, sudden and uncontrollable. The water mingles with my tears, but it can't wash them away. It can't wash him away. I sink to the floor, my knees drawn to my chest, letting the grief run through me. There's no stopping it, no escaping it. It's like being caught in a riptide, and no matter how hard I fight, it pulls me under again and again.

Why did you have to leave me, Julian?

When I finally drag myself out of the shower, I avoid the mirror. I don't need to look. I already know what I'll see. Hollow eyes, skin too pale, lips that don't remember how to smile. For a second, I catch a glimpse of my reflection and wish I hadn't. The person staring back is a stranger. I don't even recognize myself anymore. I look away quickly.

I tug on some clothes and head downstairs. The smell of chilaquiles greets me. It reminds me of Sunday mornings with Julian, when I'd be making breakfast and Julian would sneak bites straight from the pan. There's a sharp and painful feeling in my heart, threatening to bring me to my knees, but I push that feeling away.

Sara greets me with a smile when I step into the kitchen, but it doesn't reach her eyes. I sink into the chair at the kitchen table, the wood cold against my palms, and she slides a plate in front of me.

"Come algo," she urges, her voice tender yet insistent.

I nod and pick up a fork and move the food around, but I can't bring myself to take a bite. I haven't been able to eat much since that day. Most days, I force myself to take a few bites—just enough to keep Sara and Manny from worrying. But today is one of those days where nothing can fill the void. The smell of food turns my stomach, the thought of chewing makes my throat tighten, and nothing—not the warmth of the kitchen or Sara's watchful eyes—can cut through the numbness.

Sara doesn't push. Instead, she sits across from me, scrolling through her phone. The quiet hum of normalcy she's trying to create only makes the silence in my head louder.

I just want to crawl back into bed, to bury myself in the blankets and sleep. Sleep is the only place where I can escape, even if just for a little while.

I get up from the table and head back to my room. Sara calls after me, her voice laced with concern, but I don't answer. I don't even look back. I shut the bedroom door behind me, shutting her out, and crawl under the blankets.

Julian's picture sits on the nightstand, his familiar, lopsided smile staring back at me. I stare at it, a memory creeping into my mind.

It was the start of my college sophomore year, just as summer was fading into fall. The days were still warm, but the evenings carried a cool bite, hinting at the change of seasons. I had just finished my last class of the day and was walking back to my dorm, headphones on, scrolling through my phone to pick the next song.

The shortcut home took me past the soccer field, but I barely glanced at the players as I walked by. I wasn't paying attention. Not to them. Not to anything. I didn't hear the warning shouts—just a sudden, sharp force hitting the center of my forehead.

Pain radiated through my skull, hot and throbbing. I stumbled, stunned, and pressed my hand to the spot, wincing as the sting deepened. It took me a moment to realize what had happened. A soccer ball had hit me square in the forehead.

Embarrassment burned in my cheeks as I looked up at the field. A group of players stood frozen, their faces a mix of shock and apology. My first instinct was to glare at them, angry and humiliated, but before I could say anything, I saw him.

A guy was running toward me, his long strides closing the distance quickly. He was saying something, but his words didn't reach me. Then I remembered—I still had my headphones on.

I pulled them down, letting them rest on my shoulders just as he reached me. "Hey, are you okay? We were trying to get your attention, but you couldn't hear us," he said, both breathless and concerned.

He towered over me—easily over six feet, his broad shoulders and athletic build almost intimidating. His golden-brown skin glowed in the fading sunlight, and his hair had a subtle wave that caught the breeze. Then he smiled, a crooked, lopsided smile that completely disarmed me.

Just like that, I forgot I was upset. His presence had a way of pulling me in, making the pain—and everything else—fade into the background.

The memory dissolves, leaving only the quiet emptiness of my room. I let out a shaky breath, my chest tightening as I glance back at Julian's picture on the nightstand. His smile is still there, frozen in time, but the warmth it once gave me is now like a ghost.

I can't keep looking at him.

I roll over, turning my back to the photo, pulling the blanket tighter around me. But no matter how I position myself, I can still feel the weight of his absence pressing down on me, sharp and unrelenting.

I close my eyes, wishing for sleep, for dreams—anything to escape the ache of reality.

CHAPTER 3

I'm running, but I don't know if I'm running toward something or away from it. All I know is that fear grips me. Am I afraid of what's chasing me, or am I terrified I'll never reach whatever I'm searching for? I don't know.

The sky above is a fiery orange, almost red, as if the world itself is burning. The air feels heavy, thick with heat, and the only sound is my ragged breathing, loud and uneven, as if I've been running forever.

"Chave! Help me!"

I stop so suddenly that I nearly stumble, my heart slamming against my ribs. That voice. I know that voice. Julian.

Chave. It's what he used to call me, his nickname for me. Nobody else called me that besides him.

"Julian?!" I yell, spinning in place, my eyes scanning the endless fields that stretch out around me.

Mountains loom in the distance, their jagged peaks hazy and distorted in the orange glow. The fields are vast and empty, the tall grass swaying in waves that seem to breathe with the wind. I turn in circles, but there's no one. No movement. Nothing. Just me.

"Julian!" I scream again, the sound tearing from my throat, raw and desperate.

"Chave!"

His voice again—closer this time. My breath catches, and then I see it. There's a figure in the distance.

My body reacts before I can think. I run toward him, pumping my arms, my legs straining as if sheer effort alone could close the gap between us.

"Julian! I'm coming!" I shout, my voice trembling with equal parts of hope and terror.

Tears stream down my face, hot, blurring my vision. Fear grips me tighter with every step—not fear of what's behind me, but fear of failing, fear of not reaching him in time.

The ground beneath me shudders. The sky flickers, and cracks split through the horizon like glass about to shatter.

"No!" I scream, reaching out toward him as the world begins to fall apart. The fields dissolve into nothingness, the fiery sky collapses in on itself, and then I'm falling.

I jolt awake, gasping for air, my heart hammering in my chest. My face is damp, and it takes me a moment to realize why—tears are streaming down my cheeks.

I sit up, wiping at my face with trembling hands. If those are the dreams I'm going to be having, I don't want to dream. I push myself out of bed and head downstairs, unable to stay in my room.

Sara is in the kitchen, her back to me, busy stirring something over the stove. The scent of garlic and onion fills the air, but I barely notice it. The sunlight streaming through the windows tells me it must be late afternoon—dinnertime, maybe.

The sound of my footsteps makes her turn. Concern flashes across her face the moment she sees me, her brow furrowing. I must look terrible.

"Elle, ¿estás bien?" she asks softly. I can see the restraint in her body, the way she keeps herself from rushing to me. She's giving me space, afraid that if she moves too quickly, I'll bolt or shut her out completely.

"Sí … no… no sé." My voice cracks, flustered and uneven. I hesitate for a moment, then blurt out, "Sara, how soon can we get those sleeping pills?"

Her expression tightens, worry flickering in her eyes. I'm afraid she'll fight me on this if I'm asking so suddenly. But she doesn't. Instead, she nods slowly.

"I'll ask Manny to swing by Tia Sofía's house on his way home."

"And when is that?" I ask, my tone sharper than I mean it to be. The words come out impatient, bordering on desperate, but I can't stop myself.

Sara takes a cautious step toward me, her hands raised slightly as if to reassure me. "He gets back in three days," she says carefully.

Three days.

I feel the tension snap in my chest, frustration bubbling up and spilling over. "Three days?" I repeat, my voice rising. "That's too long."

Sara's face softens, her worry etched deep into her features. "I know, Elle. But it's the earliest he can come home. He had to make sure he left everything in order before moving out here. Just... try to hold on until then, okay?"

I shake my head, an exaggerated sigh escaping me. Three days feels like an eternity. Too long. Too much time to think, to dream, to feel everything I don't want to feel.

I take a step back, then another, widening the space between us. Sara doesn't follow, but her eyes stay locked on mine, her concern heavy and unspoken. "Elle ..." she begins, but I'm already turning away.

"I'm fine," I mutter, cutting her off as I head back to my room.

The door shuts behind me with a soft click, and the silence in the room rushes in like a wave. I stand there for a moment, staring at nothing, my hands clenched into fists at my sides.

Three days. How am I supposed to get through three more days of this?

I crawl back into bed, pulling the blanket over me like armor, but it does nothing to block out the thoughts circling in my head. The dream is still fresh in my mind— Julian's voice calling for me, his figure just out of reach. I feel so helpless.

I peek out from under the blanket, the cool air brushing against my face. I turn to look at Julian's picture. I grab it from the nightstand, holding it tight to my chest. I close my eyes.

Three days. Just three days.

CHAPTER 4

Three days later, Manny finally shows up. I greet him at the door, eager for what I know he's brought me. He pulls me into a hug, tight and lingering a little too long. When he steps back, he presses a small pill bottle into my hand. My thin fingers curl around it, feeling its weight. Finally, I can rest.

That night, I take one pill, just as the label says. Lying in bed, I stare at the ceiling, waiting for it to take effect. The house is far from quiet. Faint voices drift up from downstairs, sharp and muffled. Manny and Sara are arguing. I could probably guess what it's about, but I don't care enough to listen.

Before long, the pill begins to pull me under.

Suddenly, I'm standing at my grandma's black metal door in Mexico, the one that opens to the small courtyard of her house. The sun blazes overhead, its heat pressing down on my skin. In the distance, dogs bark, their howls blending with the impatient honking of car horns from the busy street nearby.

"Vamos, apurémonos. Ya nos agarró la tarde," my grandma says, her voice brisk as she locks the door with practiced swiftness. Her hands, steady and sure, twist the rusted key until the padlock clicks shut.

I stand on the uneven street, waiting. When she finishes, she loops her arm through mine, leaning on me for balance as we begin to walk.

We make our way down a few quiet streets. The air smells faintly of wet stone and laundry soap, reminders of freshly scrubbed courtyards hidden behind closed gates.

Then we reach the main avenue, alive with energy. The air here is thicker, richer—filled with the mingling aromas of Mexican street food. The sizzling of carne asada, tangy tamales steaming in their husks, and the faint sweetness of churros frying in oil. Vendors call out their wares, their voices ringing above the hum of the crowd. Shoppers haggle over prices. People shout greetings to one another, their words warm and familiar, as the sound of laughter ripples through the busy street.

My grandma pulls me along, stopping to buy a few things from the vendors. As we move through the crowd, a strange feeling prickles at the back of my neck. I glance over my shoulder and see a man. A stranger. He's standing a little too far away for me to make out his features, but he's watching us.

I tell myself it's nothing. Just another face in the crowd. But every time we turn a corner, he's there, lingering at the edge of my vision. He's keeping his distance, but it's deliberate. I know he wants me to see him.

"Abuela," I say softly, my voice trembling. "Apurémonos." I try to quicken our pace, but my grandma only moves slower, dragging her feet as she leans heavier on my arm.

The pit of my stomach churns as fear begins to brew. The stranger is still there, his presence a shadow at my back. I want to run, but I can't leave her behind. I don't know what to do.

Then, without warning, I turn a corner—and my grandma is gone.

The world shifts. The warm, bustling day darkens, clouds rolling in to block out the sun. The noises of the street—the vendors' calls, the laughter, the clamor of the crowd—fade into silence. All that remains is me and the stranger.

He stands there, motionless, his figure blurry and undefined. I can't see his face, but I feel his gaze, heavy and oppressive.

I turn and run, darting down one street and then another. The uneven cobblestones trip me up, but I keep going. I hide behind walls, duck into alleys, but it doesn't matter. No matter where I go, no matter how fast I run, he's there. Always there. Just far enough away to keep me guessing, but close enough to keep me trapped in his orbit.

The fear festers, growing cold and sharp, until it consumes me.

I wake up with sweat dampening my forehead, my chest heaving as I struggle to catch my breath. The dream slips away the moment I open my eyes, dissolving into shadows I can't quite pin down. But one thing is clear—it wasn't pleasant. And it wasn't about Julian.

So much for sleeping pills.

I lie still for a moment, letting the thrum of my heartbeat slow as I stare at the dark ceiling. A faint gray light leaks through the blinds, signaling the early edges of dawn. It's too early to be awake, but too late to go back to sleep.

The house is quiet, the silence feels heavier than noise. I rub my damp palms against the sheets and sit up, swinging my legs over the edge of the bed. The pills were supposed to help—weren't they? They were supposed to make it easier to sleep, to escape.

I stand and shuffle to the bathroom, my steps heavy, dragging. The cold tile stings my bare feet as I flip on the light. I turn the faucet on and splash cold water on my face, deliberately avoiding looking at the mirror. The shock jolts me awake. I accidentally look up and catch a glimpse of myself, but I don't linger too long. I look exhausted, I look like I aged a few years.

When I straighten, the pill bottle catches my eye where I left it by the sink. Its white plastic gleams under the fluorescent light. I pick it up, turning it over in my hands. One pill. As directed. That was supposed to be enough.

I unscrew the cap, staring down at the tiny white ovals inside. They seem so harmless, so ordinary. These little pills had promised me what I wanted. Rest. Escape. Silence. But they've failed to keep their promise. I feel as empty as I did the day before.

With a sigh,I screw the cap back on and set the bottle down.

Back in my room, the bed feels too big, too empty. I stand at its edge for several long seconds, hesitating, before finally slipping under the covers. The sheets are cool against my skin. I stare at the ceiling, my body exhausted, yet unable to surrender to sleep.

My mind keeps going back to the dream. Something about it keeps tugging at me, like a thread I'm afraid to pull.

I don't know how long I lie there before the first rays of sunlight break through the blinds. I can hear birds chirping faintly outside, their songs faint. A reminder that the world keeps moving.

I close my eyes. And this time, slowly I drift back to sleep on my own.

CHAPTER 5

The days begin to blur together, one bleeding into the next. I've been taking sleeping pills every other night. They seem to be doing what they're supposed to do. Keep me from dreaming. Without the dreams, I don't wake up gasping for air or clawing at memories that slip away the moment I reach for them. It's almost like they're dulling the edges of my grief, easing some of the weight.

But the emptiness is still there. It greets me every morning, heavy and unshakable. Dragging myself out of bed feels like fighting a current, my body moving while my mind stays behind. I go through the motions of the day mechanically. Everything feels distant, like I'm watching someone else's life unfold.

Manny and Sara try their best to help, to give me some semblance of normalcy. Manny doesn't push my limits, but he has his ways of letting me know he's there. He checks in with short conversations, leaves my favorite snacks on the counter—even though I don't touch them. Sara, on the other hand, hovers constantly. She makes sure I get a few bites of food, starts conversations I rarely hear, her voice little more than background noise. They're both trying to fill the void, but the truth is, it's unfillable.

I count the hours until I can finally crawl back into bed, until I can surrender to the dark abyss of nothing. In that nothingness, I don't feel anything. No grief. No memories. No pain. Just silence. And I crave that.

Tonight isn't any different. When 9 p.m. finally rolls around, I excuse myself and head into my cold, dark room. I don't even bother showering, brushing my teeth, or changing out of my lounging clothes. I just slip under the covers and wait for sleep to take me.

It doesn't take long. These days, I don't even need the sleeping pills to fall asleep. I'm always tired. Exhausted in a way that feels bone-deep, as though every part of me has given up. But I still take the pills—not because I need them to sleep, but because without them, I dream. And I can't bear the dreams.

Tonight is one of the nights I don't take them. Still, sleep comes easily, pulling me under like the tide.

I find myself standing in front of Julian's tombstone. The sky is heavy with dark clouds, thunder rumbling faintly in the distance. The air feels damp, charged. I don't like this. Whispers float on the wind, faint, tugging at my ears. I turn in slow circles, searching for the source, but I'm completely alone.

"*¡Es tu culpa!*"

My head snaps to the right, my pulse spiking. It's her voice. My mother-in-law's. For a moment, I expect to see her there, her face twisted in anger, but there's nobody.

"It should have been you!"

This time, the voice comes from my left. But it isn't hers. It's mine.

I spin around as a figure steps out of the shadows, the shape unfamiliar at first. But as it moves closer. I take in a sharp breath. It's me. A twisted, sinister version of me. Her mouth stretches into a grin, sharp and cruel, malice dripping from each corner.

I try to speak, but no sound comes out. I try to move, but my feet feel glued to the ground.

"It should have been you, Isabella," she says, her voice calm but hollow, like the scrape of cold metal. "Julian had his whole life ahead of him. He had people who loved him. His parents. His siblings. His friends. What do you have?"

The figure inches closer, her movements eerily smooth, her grin never wavering. "You have no parents. No friends. Where are those family members who said they'd always be there for you? You have no one. It should have been you."

Her lips don't move as she speaks, yet the words fill the air, echoing all around me.

The air grows colder. I shiver as icy tendrils curl around my skin. I want to turn, to run, but my feet are frozen in place, rooted in the cold, damp dirt beneath me.

The thunder grows louder now, reverberating through my chest. A jagged streak of lightning splits the sky, illuminating the figure in front of me. She's still grinning, but her eyes they're black, two empty voids that swallow the light.

I can't move. I can't breathe. All I can do is watch as she gets closer, her steps slow and deliberate, until she's mere inches from me.

"What do you have to say for yourself, you worthless bitch?" she hisses, her head tilting unnaturally to the side, her grin growing even wider.

I swallow hard, forcing the lump in my throat down. "You're right. It should have been me. Julian was always the better person. He was like the sun, brightening everyone's day just by being there. But you're wrong. I'm not alone! I have Manny and Sara, and they love me. They love me very much!"

Her grin falters for a split second, but then another voice cuts through the darkness.

"Are you sure about that, hermanita?"

The voice is unmistakable. My heart stops. It's Manny.

I whip my head around, my stomach dropping as I see him step out of the shadows. But this isn't *my* Manny. No, no this Manny has no soul in his eyes. There is no emotion on his face.

"Ma … Ma … Manny," I stammer, my voice cracking.

"You could have saved us all the trouble of uprooting our lives for you," says another voice.

It's Sara's.

I turn toward the sound, and another figure emerges from the darkness. It's Sara. But it's not *my* Sara. Her expression is eerily blank, her head tilted just slightly to the side, the way a doll might tilt if it were broken. Her eyes, empty of recognition, lock onto me.

"But … I …" The words catch in my throat. I don't know what to say. My chest tightens, and tears spill from my eyes as I look between the three of them—Manny, Sara, and the twisted version of myself.

My sinister self steps closer. Her grin widens, stretching unnaturally, nearly reaching her eyes. Her teeth, bright and impossibly white, gleam in the dim light. There's something deeply wrong about the way her face twists, the grin a distorted imitation of human expression.

I still can't move.

Before I can process what's happening, they all reach for me—Manny, Sara, and my other self. Their hands are cold, skeletal, their fingers curling around my arms, my shoulders, my neck. With one forceful shove, they push me backward.

I fall hard, the air rushing from my lungs as I hit the ground with a dull, sickening thud.

My eyes squeeze shut on instinct, but when I open them, I'm no longer standing on solid ground.

I'm in a pit.

The damp walls rise around me, their surfaces slick with mud. I scramble to sit up, my palms slipping against the dirt. When I look up, I see them—Manny, Sara, and myself.

They're staring down at me from the edge of the pit, their faces distorted by those same unnatural grins. Teeth bared. Eyes empty. Soulless.

And then, as if they're sharing some silent joke, they start laughing.

The sound is wrong. It echoes unnaturally, sharp and grating, like metal scraping against glass. It drills into my skull, reverberating through my chest, rattling my bones. I press my hands over my ears, but it doesn't stop. It grows louder, more relentless.

Then, dirt begins to fall.

At first, it's just a sprinkle, loose bits of soil raining down on my hair, my shoulders. But then it comes in clumps, heavy and cold, hitting my arms, my legs. My stomach clenches as the horrifying realization sets in.

They're burying me.

"No! Please, no!" I scream as I claw desperately at the sides of the pit. My nails scrape against the mud, breaking off as I try to find something to grip, something to pull myself out. But it's useless. The walls are too wet, too slippery.

"Don't fight it, Isabella," a voice says, smooth and cold.

I freeze. I don't recognize the voice. It isn't Manny, Sara, or even my sinister self. It's something else. Someone else.

"You know you don't want to live anyway," the voice continues, calm and casual, as if it's stating an obvious fact. "So let us help you."

The laughter above me swells, mingling with the voice, growing louder and louder until it's all I can hear. The dirt keeps falling, heavier now, covering my legs, my arms. Panic floods my chest, and I try to scream again, but the sound is swallowed by the choking weight of soil filling the air around me.

"No!" I scream, bolting upright in my bed.

My chest heaves as I gasp for air. My heart pounds violently against my ribs, my skin slick with sweat. I clutch the blankets tightly in trembling fists. For a moment, I can't tell if I'm still in the nightmare or if I've woken up at all.

The bedroom door flies open, and Manny bursts in, his face etched with panic.

"Elle, what's wrong?" he asks, rushing to my side and turning on the lamp on my nightstand to get a better look at me.

I open my mouth to answer, but the words won't come. My mind is still tangled in the dream, the echoes of the voice and the laughter lingering in my ears like ghosts.

Sara appears a few seconds later, her hair disheveled, worry carving its way into her features.

"¿Qué pasó?" she asks, hurrying to my other side. Her hand touches my shoulder lightly and I flinch at her touch.

Sara lets her hand fall near mine without touching it. Guilt twists in my chest. Did I hurt her feelings by flinching? Her expression doesn't give anything way, but the way she's hesitating speaks louder than words.

I glance at her, then at Manny. They look like the siblings I know and love. The ones who care about me. The ones who would do anything for me.

Are you sure about that?

The thought slithers into my mind, uninvited, and I push it away.

"I …" I stammer, my voice unsteady as I fight to calm my racing heart. "I had a really terrible nightmare."

"You scared me. I thought something bad had happened to you," Manny says, his voice laced with annoyance.

"I'm … I'm sorry," I whisper, my eyes dropping to my hands. Shame prickles at the back of my neck. I shouldn't have woken them up in the middle of the night.

"It's okay, Elle. As long as you're okay," Sara says softly, shooting Manny a pointed look that makes him shift uncomfortably. She moves closer, her voice gentle. "Do you want me to stay with you?"

I shake my head quickly, already feeling like a burden. "No, I'll be okay. You guys go back to bed. You have to work in the morning."

"You're sure?" Sara asks, her brow furrowed in concern.

"Yes. I promise," I say.

Manny exhales loudly, clearly relieved to return to his room. "Okay, but call us if you need anything," he mutters before turning and heading toward the door.

Sara lingers a moment longer, her eyes searching mine. I try to give her my best *I'll be fine* look, willing for her to believe it. It must have worked because she gives me a nod and follows Manny out, closing the door behind her.

Silence settles over the room, a little too heavy.

I sit there in the quiet, the weight of the nightmare pressing against me. I pull my knees to my chest, hugging them tightly as I try to shake the lingering echo of the laughter, the dirt, the voice.

It should have been you.

The words hit me like a blow, as piercing and cruel as they were in the dream. My throat tightens, and tears spill from my eyes before I can stop them. I press my hand over my mouth to stifle the sobs that rise, desperate not to make a sound. I don't want Manny or Sara to come back in and see me like this—broken, unraveling.

But they're right …

The tears fall harder now.

It should have been me.

CHAPTER 6

I wake to the sun peeking through the curtains, casting a soft glow, a contrast to how I'm feeling.

I exhale shakily, sitting up in bed and hugging my knees to my chest. Last night's nightmare left me feeling …hollow. Undeserving. A burden.

The memory of the dirt hitting my body, the helplessness of being buried alive comes rushing back. My chest tightens as I remember the sensation and grip the blanket as tightly as I can as if it can keep me steady.

It should have been you.

I shake my head, trying to force the thought away, but it clings to me.

I glance at the door, half expecting Manny or Sara to check in on me, but the house is silent. They must have already left for work. Part of me is relieved, grateful for the space, but another part feels … empty.

I drag myself out of bed, each movement sluggish and stiff. The familiar ache settles into my bones, the kind that tells me today will be another uphill battle just to exist. My feet hit the cold floor, and I shuffle to the window.

The neighborhood outside looks so normal. A dog barks somewhere in the distance. A man jogs past, earbuds in, oblivious to the fact that I'm standing here, barely holding myself together.

I press my forehead against the cool glass, closing my eyes. Hoping that the sun itself is enough to warm the coldness I feel inside. But it doesn't.

When I open my eyes, I tilt my head back towards the nightstand where Julian's picture rests. I walk back to it, picking up the frame.

I study his face. His crooked smile, always a little lopsided, a smile that could disarm anyone. That smile had a way of lighting up his dark brown eyes, making them sparkle with mischief and warmth. But now that smile is frozen in time, trapped in a photograph.

I trace his face with my fingers, longing to feel the warmth of his skin, the softness of his cheek beneath my touch. But it's just glass. There's no warmth.

A memory creeps in, slow and bittersweet.

"Isabella Garcia, I'm going to marry you one day," Julian said, sitting across from me at a table, a spoonful of ice cream in his hand.

It was the beginning of summer. We'd been dating for just over six months, and we'd both decided to take summer classes. He'd met me after my last class to grab ice cream, the day too perfect to waste indoors. We sat outside on the patio of the little ice cream shop, the sun filtered through the tree's leaves overhead.

I remember choking on my ice cream, startled. "Excuse me?" I asked, flustered, my cheeks heating under his gaze.

Julian laughed, a sound so rich and carefree it drew the attention of a couple sitting nearby. "You heard me. I'm going to marry you," he said, his dark eyes dancing with mischief.

"¡Estás loco!" I shot back, shaking my head at him. "We've only been dating …" I stopped to count the months on my fingers. "A little over six months! You can't say stuff like that! What if I don't want to marry you?"

My words only made him laugh harder. "Oh, you will," he said, his confidence unwavering.

And he was right.

God, I would give anything to hear his voice again. To feel his touch. To be with him.

There is a way.

The thought crosses my mind, dark and unbidden, sending a chill down my spine. For a moment, I let it linger, its pull as tempting as it is terrifying.

"No," I whisper to myself, shaking my head as though I can physically dislodge the idea. I set the picture frame back on the nightstand, carefully, as though it might shatter in my hands.

I close my eyes and take a few deep breaths, trying to calm my nervous system. But it doesn't help.

Dragging my feet, I make my way to the door and then downstairs, each step feeling heavier than the last. By the time I reach the living room, I let myself collapse into the couch, sinking into its cushions like they might swallow me whole.

The house is quiet.

The only sound is the steady ticking of the clock on the wall, each tick slicing through the silence like a tiny reminder of how slowly time crawls. The blinds are open, and I stare out onto the street, watching as life moves on without me. Cars pass by. A group of kids run while laughing.

I don't even know what time it is. I stopped checking. Why bother? Every day feels the same—an endless cycle with no beginning and no end.

A car door slams outside, and a few minutes later, the front door creaks open.

"Elle?" Manny's voice breaks the silence.

I don't bother to answer, but I turn my head just enough for him to see that I heard him.

He steps into the room, looking at me with a furrowed brow before heading to the entry closet to put his things away. "What have you been doing?" he asks over his shoulder.

"Nothing," I reply flatly, turning my attention back to the window.

Manny walks back into the living room, standing a few inches from the couch. "Where's Sara? She usually beats me home."

"I don't know," I say, my tone edged with annoyance.

The truth is, I haven't been paying attention. I don't know when Manny and Sara leave for work or when they come home. Most days, they're already gone by the time I drag myself out of bed, or Sara is here, hovering. She's always trying to get me to eat something, go outside for some fresh air, or do the bare minimum—shower, brush my teeth, change out of the same clothes I've been wearing for days.

All I know is that every day feels the same.

Manny watches me for a long moment, his expression unreadable. I can feel his frustration, though—it's there in the way his lips press into a thin line, the way his shoulders stiffen. But he doesn't say anything—not yet, at least. Instead, he exhales heavily, dragging a hand through his neatly styled hair, leaving it tousled and uneven, ruining his polished, professional look. Without another word, he turns and walks toward the kitchen.

"Any preference for dinner?" Manny calls out, his voice raised over the sound of him shuffling things around in the fridge.

"Not really!" I shout back, though it feels like too much effort to even respond.

Time blurs after that. Minutes, maybe hours—I can't tell. The next thing I notice is the sound of the front door opening, slamming shut again. Sara's home. Her entrance is as loud as always, a whirlwind of movement and noise. She strides into the living room and plops down on the couch beside me, the cushions sinking under her weight.

I glance at her out of the corner of my eye. Her cheeks are flushed, and her eyes are red, like she's been crying. But I don't ask why. I don't really care.

"Sorry I'm late," Sara says, her voice slightly strained. She grabs the remote and turns on the TV without looking at me. "I had to take care of something."

Manny walks into the room a moment later, wiping his hands on a dish towel. "I hope enchiladas are okay. You weren't answering your phone, and chicken was the only thing that wasn't frozen. I couldn't think of anything else to make," he says, glancing between Sara and me.

Sara mumbles something in response, and Manny starts talking about … something. I'm not sure. I'm not listening. Their voices feel like background noise, distant and muffled.

I'm so tired. Exhausted, really. But the thought of falling asleep again terrifies me. What if I have another nightmare?

Wait—today I can take a sleeping pill.

"Elle?" Sara's voice cuts through the haze, snapping me back to the present.

"What?" I ask, blinking at her.

"I asked if you ate today," she says, her frustration evident despite the careful way she's trying to mask it.

"Um … No, I don't think I did," I mumble, glancing down at my lap.

Sara lets out a sharp, exasperated sigh, raking a hand through her long wavy hair. "Okay, well, you need to eat something. Come on, dinner's ready," she says, standing up from the couch. She offers me her hand, holding it out in a way that leaves no room for argument.

I stare at her hand for a moment, hesitating. Part of me doesn't want to move, doesn't want to leave this couch. But her eyes are locked on mine, unyielding, and I know she won't let this go. Reluctantly, I reach out and take her hand, letting her pull me to my feet.

At the kitchen table, I force a few bites down, chewing mechanically under Sara's watchful gaze. Once she's satisfied—when I've eaten just enough for her to let me go—I push back my chair and mumble a quiet, "Goodnight."

I don't wait for a response. I slip away, climbing the stairs back to my room, back to the silence.

Inside the bathroom, I open the medicine cabinet and reach for the pill bottle. I unscrew the lid. I shake out one of the small white pills and stare at it for a moment before placing it on my tongue. I swallow it dry.

I glance back down at the bottle. The pills rattle softly as I tip the container from side to side, my thumb brushing over the label. For a fleeting moment, the thought crosses my mind—*What if I just took another?*

But I don't.

I twist the lid back on, placing the bottle back where I found it. Turning off the bathroom light, I retreat to my bed, crawling under the covers and pulling them around me.

I close my eyes, waiting for sleep to come.

This time there is complete darkness.

CHAPTER 7

"Elle."

I hear my name in the distance, faint and muffled.

"Elle."

The sound comes again, sharper this time, cutting through the fog in my mind. Then I feel a gentle shake.

"Elle!"

My eyes snap open.

The room comes into focus slowly, shapes swimming in the soft morning light. Sara is leaning over me, her hand on my shoulder, concern etched across her face.

"You scared me," she says, her voice low.

I rub my eyes and push myself upright, groggy and disoriented. "Sorry … the sleeping pill really knocked me out this time," I mumble, my voice thick with sleep.

Sara hesitates, her lips parting as though she wants to say something. "Elle …" she begins but stops herself. Her expression shifts, like she's debating whether to continue. Instead she says, "Your phone's been ringing. It's Emily."

I blink at her, confused. Emily? My brow furrows as I try to remember the last time I even saw my phone.

"I've been keeping it," she says quietly, as if reading my mind. "In case anybody tries to reach you. I wasn't sure you'd even check it."

She reaches into her pocket and pulls out my phone, holding it out to me.

I take it hesitantly, my fingers brushing hers. The device feels foreign in my hands, its weight somehow heavier than I remember. The screen lights up, and my breath catches as I see the image displayed there—a picture of Julian and me at Tokyo Disneyland.

In the photo, we're standing in front of the castle, both of us grinning like fools. His arm is slung casually around my shoulders, and my head is tilted toward him, caught mid-laugh.

Julian had come up with the idea to go to Japan for sakura season two months before the cherry blossoms were supposed to bloom. I remember fighting with him about it—arguing that two months wasn't enough time to plan everything, that flights would be expensive, and that asking for time off from work would be a hassle. But Julian, being Julian, had convinced me like he always did.

We booked the flights on a whim, and somehow, it all came together. We ended up spending three weeks in Japan. It was one of the best trips we ever took.

The lump in my throat grows, but I swallow it down before it can take over. "Thanks," I mutter, keeping my eyes fixed on the screen to avoid looking at Sara.

She lingers for a moment, watching me. "You should call her back." She says as she turns and walks out of the room, her footsteps fading down the hall.

I sit there, the phone still in my hand, the picture of Julian and me glowing faintly in the dim light. My thumb hovers over the screen, but I can't bring myself to do anything.

I've been avoiding calls from family and friends for weeks, maybe longer. I know exactly what they'll say—it's always the same. *I'm so sorry for your loss. How are you holding up?* Then there's the awkward silence that follows, that suffocating pause when they don't know what else to say, when they stumble over their words, unsure of what's appropriate.

I'd rather not deal with it. Any of it.

If shutting them out means I don't have to endure their pity or discomfort, then so be it. I don't care.

With a flick of my wrist, I toss my phone across the bed. It lands with a muted thud against the blankets, face down.

Sliding back under the covers, I pull them up to my chin. I stare up at the ceiling, my thoughts swirling, but I'm too tired to chase them.

I'm too tired to do anything.

Too tired to exist.

There's a way out. A way to see Julian again.

The thought cuts through my mind so suddenly, so intensely, that it almost doesn't feel like it's mine.

What if I could be with Julian again?

The idea expands in my mind, dark and seductive.

I could escape all of this pain.

I curl into myself, pulling my knees to my chest and wrapping my arms around them as tightly as I can.

The ache is unbearable, clawing at the edges of me, consuming everything. If there really is a way out of this, I'll take it.

CHAPTER 8

I wake up with the dark thoughts still lingering, hovering at the edges of my mind, whispering tempting promises I can't quite ignore.

I force myself out of bed, my limbs heavy and uncooperative, and stumble toward the stairs. Each step feels like dragging my body through quicksand.

Downstairs, I find Sara darting between the kitchen and the living room. The faint smell of coffee drifts through the air. It used to be one of my favorite smells. Now, it barely registers.

I grab the blanket draped over the couch's armrest and wrap it around my shoulders, sinking into the cushions.

"Elle, I have to leave early today." Sara says as she darts back into the living room. "Manny will be back in about twenty minutes. Will you be okay?"

She's asking a simple question, but the concern beneath her words is impossible to miss. I don't want to answer, so I do what I always do—I try to avoid it. Mustering what I hope is a halfhearted smile, I nod.

Sara hesitates for a moment, watching me like she's debating whether to press further, but then she turns and disappears into the kitchen again.

A thought flickers across my mind, unexpected, igniting a small, almost eager spark inside me. I sit up a little straighter, feeling the pull of it, even as shame nips at the edges.

"Hey, Sara," I call out, trying to keep my voice steady. I pause, gathering the courage I need. "Can you do me a favor?"

She walks back into the living room, glancing at me over the rim of her mug.

"Could you ask Tía Sofía if she can get me more sleeping pills?" I try to make the request sound casual, like it's no big deal, like I'm asking her to pick up milk or bread.

Sara freezes for half a second. It's barely noticeable, but I catch it. Slowly, she lowers the mug from her lips and steps closer.

Her eyes narrow slightly as she studies me. "Elle, don't you think you should cut back on those? They help you sleep, sure, but it's been a month. Maybe we should ... I don't know, look at other options? We're worried about you."

They're always tiptoeing around me, Manny and Sara. Like I'm some fragile thing, on the verge of cracking if they press too hard.

But I'm more broken than they realize.

Broken beyond repair.

And no amount of tiptoeing or worrying will change that.

I can't see how I'm supposed to come back from this.

I look down at my hands, picking at the skin around my nails. "It's just for a little longer," I say, my voice low but steady. "I promise, after this refill, we can talk about other options."

I try to sound convincing, to make it seem like I believe what I'm saying. But deep down, I know I'm lying.

There will be no alternatives. No other options.

I've been circling the same dark thought for days now, and with each passing hour, it grows louder, sharper, more certain.

The only real solution is within reach. I just haven't had the chance.

Not yet.

Until today.

Sara studies me, her eyes scanning my face as if trying to read my mind. The silence stretches between us, thick with unspoken worry.

After what feels like an eternity, she sighs and shakes her head. "Fine. How can I say no to my baby sister? You're lucky I love you."

Her words should be comforting, but they only tighten the knot of guilt in my stomach. I push it down and force a small, brittle smile. "Thank you, Sara. I love you, too."

She returns a sad smile, one that doesn't quite reach her eyes. "I'll call Tía Sofía. Do you have enough for this week?"

I nod quickly, my voice barely above a whisper. "Yeah, I still have some left."

She hesitates, eyes searching mine one last time, as if looking for reassurance. "I left some food for you. Are you sure you'll be okay?"

I nod, avoiding her eyes.

Once Sara leaves, silence settles around the house. I've gotten used to it but today it feels different. It's as if it's reminding me I have to move fast before I change my mind or before I lose out on this opportunity that I've been waiting for.

I rush upstairs, my heart pounding harder with each step. The bathroom feels colder than usual, or maybe that's just me. I pull open the medicine cabinet, my reflection flickering in the mirror as the door swings wide.

The pills are right where I left them.

With trembling hands, I grab the bottle and twist the cap. My palms are slick, my fingers clumsy. The bottle slips from my grasp and tumbles onto the counter.

Tiny white tablets scatter everywhere, bouncing and rolling like beads across the surface.

I freeze, staring at the mess, but I remind myself there's no time.

I sweep as many pills as I can into my hand and shove them into my mouth, their bitterness spreading across my tongue. My hands shake as I turn on the faucet, gulping down enough water to swallow them.

That should be enough.

I stagger back into my bedroom, grabbing Julian's picture from the nightstand. My knees give out, and I sink to the floor, leaning against the bed. I clutch the photo to my chest, my fingers brushing against the glass, as if it's his face I'm touching.

"Pronto, mi amor," I whisper, my voice trembling. "Vamos a estar juntos."

The world begins to blur, the edges of my vision darkening. My breathing slows, shallow and uneven. Just as the darkness starts to pull me under, I see it—a light.

Far away at first, faint, like a pinprick in a tunnel. But it grows, brightening, coming closer.

My breath hitches.

Julian.

He's there, standing in the light. But something's wrong. His expression isn't the warm, loving one I remember. It's filled with worry.

"Chave, amor. Hold on! You have to hold on!"

His voice is frantic, desperate in a way I've never heard before. It cuts through the fog creeping over my mind, sharper than any thought.

Chave. That's what he used to call me.

I want to answer him, to tell him how much I miss him, how much I love him, but my throat feels tight. The words won't come. The world spins around me, the pills gripping harder, dragging me deeper into the abyss.

"Hold on, amor! Help is coming!"

My chest tightens as panic flares. What have I done?

Julian! I want to scream, but no sound escapes my lips. My limbs feel heavy, impossible to move. My heart thunders in my chest, but it feels far away, like it belongs to someone else.

Julian, please. Help me!

Through the fog, another voice breaks through. It's distant at first, but it grows louder, more frantic.

Manny.

I hear him calling my name, his voice thick with terror. His cries echo in my mind. Gulit sears through me.

I never meant to hurt him. I never meant to hurt them.

How could I do this to them?

I want to claw my way out, to take it back, to reverse everything. But I can't. It's too late.

Julian's face is the last thing I see, his dark eyes locked on mine, his expression full of anguish.

"You need to live, Chave," he says, his voice soft, breaking, before the light fades and I'm swallowed whole by the darkness.

CHAPTER 9

When I finally surface from the murky depths of unconsciousness, reality cuts through me, cold and merciless. The sharp smell of antiseptic stings my nose, and the stiff sheets beneath me scratch against my skin. Blinking away the haze, I find myself staring up at the harsh, fluorescent lights. The rhythmic beeping of the machines nearby reminds me that I'm still alive.

I stay still, letting the coldness of the room seep into my bones.

The last thing I remember is Julian—his face, his voice. His words echo in my mind, clear and unrelenting. *Hold on, Chave. You have to live.*

I don't know how, but I am.

I'm alive.

But instead of feeling relief, all I feel is guilt. Heavy, suffocating guilt that presses hard against my ribs, making it impossible to breathe.

I turn my head slightly, and my gaze lands on Sara, curled awkwardly in the chair beside me. Her body is twisted at an unnatural angle, her head tilted back against the chair, her arm dangling off the side. Even in sleep, her face is etched with exhaustion, her features tight, like she's been carrying the weight of the world on her shoulders.

I close my eyes and exhale slowly.

What have I done?

The muffled sounds of voices and distant footsteps outside blur into the background, fading into static.

The door slides open with a soft hiss, and I force my eyes open again. Manny steps into the room, his broad frame silhouetted against the harsh light from the hallway. For a moment, he just stands there, his eyes fixed on me. When our gazes meet, the look on his face makes my heart plummet—relief tangled with concern, like he's holding onto me with both hands, terrified I might slip away again.

"Isabella!" he breathes, his voice cracking slightly as it cuts through the sterile silence. "You're awake!"

His voice jolts Sara awake. She sits up with a sharp gasp, her eyes wide and frantic for half a second before they land on me. Relief washes over her face, softening her features as she scrambles to her feet.

In an instant, they're both at my bedside, hovering like I'm made of glass.

Their faces are alive with emotions I don't deserve.

Relief. Concern. Even happiness.

It's too much. My chest tightens, and tears burn at the edges of my vision. Their blurry forms merge as I choke out the words I've been holding in since I woke up.

"I'm sorry," I croak, my voice barely more than a whisper. "I'm so sorry."

Before I can say more, Sara's arms are around me, pulling me into a fierce embrace. She's trembling, her tears hot against my skin as she holds me like I'll disappear if she lets go.

"Don't," she whispers, her voice breaking. "Don't apologize. Just … don't leave us. Please."

Manny steps closer, wrapping his arms around both of us. His grip is steady and strong, grounding us in this fragile moment.

The three of us cling to each other—a tangled mess of tears, apologies, and silent promises.

And in the middle of it all, I make a vow.

To them. To myself. To Julian's memory.

Never again.

CHAPTER 10

I'm released from the hospital the next day, after a series of evaluations. Once the doctors decide I'm no longer a danger to myself, they hand me over to Manny's care.

Manny and Sara have made it very clear that I am not to be trusted to be alone. Not until I get the help I need.

Manny rearranges his life to work remotely, always nearby, quietly keeping an eye on me. Sara has moved into my room, her presence constant, making sure I'm never alone—not even when I sleep. Between the two of them, solitude is no longer an option.

The sleeping pills are gone. They made sure of that.

Sara even made an appointment with a grief therapist—someone who specializes in depression. I didn't argue. I didn't have the strength, and deep down, I know they're scared. Scared of what I might do if left to my own devices.

Two weeks later, I find myself sitting in the quiet, air-conditioned office of Dr. Rivera. Her space is warm but clinical, decorated with soft earth tones and a single plant on the windowsill.

I stare at the plant instead of meeting her gaze, twirling my wedding ring around and around on my finger as I struggle to find the words to speak.

Dr. Rivera notices the movement, but she doesn't comment. Her expression remains neutral, her posture calm, her eyes patient. She's giving me space, I know, waiting for me to come to her on my own terms.

So far, I've only managed to answer a few basic questions. She asked me about past losses—I told her about my parents. She nodded, jotting something down in her notepad, but she didn't press further.

She's careful.

Her voice is quiet when she finally asks the question. "Can you share with me what you were doing on the day of the death?"

The words are gentle, but they hit me like a blade, sharp and precise, cutting through the protective wall I've built around my grief.

I guess we're diving straight in.

I swallow hard, my fingers tightening around my wedding ring as the memories I've worked so hard to bury resurface, pulling me under.

"I was at home," I say hesitantly, my voice barely above a whisper. "Lying on the couch, watching a rom-com while waiting for Julian to come back …" My voice trails off as the memory rushes in, sharp and vivid. My throat tightens, tears blurring my vision.

I swallow hard, trying to push the emotion down. Dr. Rivera offers me a tissue, and I take it without meeting her eyes.

"It's okay, Isabella," she says softly. "Take deep breaths. Take your time."

I do as she tells me. One breath. Two. By the third, my emotions stabilize enough to continue.

"Good," she says. "Who informed you?"

"The hospital did," I reply, the memory rushing back, vivid and unwelcome ...

The phone call had come from an unknown number, but the caller ID read *Healthcare,* so I answered.

"Hello?" I said, my voice hesitant, unsure.

"May I speak to Isabella Lopez?" a woman's calm, measured voice had asked.

I had a sinking feeling, a cold weight in my chest. Something was wrong, but I didn't want to jump to conclusions. "This is her," I said.

"We're calling because Julian Lopez is currently in the emergency room with severe injuries. We need you to come to the hospital as soon as possible."

I remember the way my stomach dropped, the way my hands trembled as I hung up the phone. I think I said something—maybe "thank you," maybe nothing at all—but I don't remember. I do remember stumbling around the house, frantically searching for my keys, my mind blank except for one desperate thought: *Get to Julian. Just get to Julian.*

"How did you react to the news?" Dr. Rivera asks, her calm voice pulling me back into the office.

Her question hits a nerve. A flicker of anger rises in my chest, sudden and sharp. *What does she expect me to say?*

"What do you mean, how did I react to the news?" The words come out louder and harsher than I intended. My jaw clenches, heat rising to my face. As soon as the outburst escapes, I regret it. I close my eyes, shame washes over me.

"I'm sorry," I mutter, twirling my wedding ring again.

"Don't be," Dr. Rivera says gently. "It's normal to feel angry. These questions might seem difficult—even frustrating—but they help me understand your emotional state. It's part of the process. It helps me help you."

Her voice is so steady, so understanding, that I risk a glance at her. When I meet her eyes, I see no judgment, only compassion.

My emotional state? What even *is* my emotional state? I feel empty—like someone scooped out the parts of me that cared and left nothing but silence. A heavy, suffocating silence. I feel like I'm stuck in a fog, watching the world go on without me, unable to reach it. Unable to care.

"What are you thinking, Isabella?"

I sigh. "I feel ... nothing. Just this emptiness. Like I'm watching my life from a distance. Nothing seems real. Nothing seems worth it."

She nods, her expression softening. "That's a normal response to grief. You've been through a trauma. It's going to take time to process all of this."

I don't respond. It's not that I don't believe her—it's that I don't *want* to believe her. What if I don't want to process it? What if this fog is safer than facing what's on the other side?

The session ends before I realize it. I find myself in the lobby, waiting for Sara to pick me up. My thoughts are tangled, a knot of things I should have said and things I'm still too afraid to say out loud.

Dr. Rivera said healing is a process. That it takes time.

But what if I'm not ready to heal?

Sara texts to say she's running late, and I promise to wait for her like she asked. But after a few minutes, the office walls feel too close, pressing in on me. I need air.

I step outside into the late afternoon sunlight, the warm air brushing gently against my skin. It's late spring— the kind of day I used to love, when the world felt alive and full of possibility.

I start walking, no destination in mind, letting my feet guide me. As I pass a glass window, my reflection stops me. I barely recognize myself. I've lost weight. My clothes hang loose, and my hair is a mess. The woman staring back at me looks haunted, like she's been drifting for years.

Turn back.

I freeze, my heart stuttering in my chest. I glance around quickly, but there's no one nearby. The street is quiet, except for the distant hum of traffic.

Did I imagine that? I take a shaky breath, forcing a nervous chuckle. Of course I did. My mind is playing tricks on me. Shaking my head, I keep walking.

Turn back.

This time the voice is louder, more insistent. I stop again, panic prickling at the edge of my mind. The voice … It's so familiar. My breath catches as realization sinks in. *Julian?*

Frustrated and unnerved, I blurt, "¡Qué chingado!"

I glance around again, feeling foolish. I'm hearing things. That's all this is. My grief is messing with my mind. It's just stress. It's nothing.

Guilt starts to rise, crushing me. If I keep walking, Sara will find an empty lobby. She'll panic. She'll think I broke my promise. I picture her face—the fear, the disappointment. I can't do that to her.

Slowly, I turn around, retracing my steps to the therapist's office.

When I reach the door, Sara's car pulls into the lot. She steps out, her face lighting up when she sees me.

I force a smile, my heart still racing. I almost kept walking. I almost broke my promise.

But I didn't.

For now, I've kept my promise to Sara and Manny.

And maybe, just maybe, that's enough.

CHAPTER 11

"Ready?" Sara checks her reflection one last time before turning to me with an eager grin.

"Almost," I reply, fastening an earring while rummaging through my cluttered makeup drawer.

"Niñas, vamos a llegar tarde! We won't get the best seats!" Manny's voice floats up from downstairs, his impatience clear.

"Ya vamos!" Sara and I shout back in unison, scrambling to grab our things before heading downstairs and out the door.

As I sling my purse over my shoulder, my phone buzzes from where I tossed it on the bed earlier. Emily. Again.

I hesitate, then snatch it up, my fingers hovering over the screen. But I don't answer. I never do.

I tell myself I'll call her back, that I just need a little more time. But the truth is, I don't know what to say. Every time I see a message—*Hey Elle, just checking in. I hope you're doing well. I miss you. Can we talk soon?*—something in my chest tightens. I don't know how to be around friends who knew Julian and me before. I need to figure out who I am again, and until I do, I can't bring myself to let them in. Especially Emily.

I feel guilty. I know I'm shutting her out, and she doesn't deserve it. But that guilt isn't enough to make me pick up the phone. Not yet. I will… when I'm ready.

It's been three months since I heard Julian's voice. I haven't told anyone about it—not even Dr. Rivera. It's not that I've forgotten; it's that I don't know how to explain it.

Since then, things have been… better, I guess. Therapy twice a week helps, and Sundays at mass with Sara and Manny give me something to hold onto. A routine. A small thread keeping me tethered to the world. Most nights, I can sleep without trouble, though grief still sneaks in when I least expect it.

But today feels different. Today feels … lighter. Almost normal.

"En el nombre del Padre, el Hijo y el Espíritu Santo. Vamos con Dios." The priest's voice echoes through the church as mass comes to a close. We stand with the crowd, slowly making our way toward the exit.

"Before we leave, we need to find Tía Lupe," Sara reminds us, her eyes darting through the crowd. "She said to meet her after mass. She has little gifts from Grandma."

Manny huffs. "Can't we just pick them up from her house later?"

"No way! I'm way too curious. I want to see what Grandma sent!" Sara insists, her enthusiasm lighting up her face.

"You know what would be even better? If you actually paid her a visit," I suggest.

"I was planning to, but ..." Sara trails off, the unspoken reason hanging in the air between us for a moment before Manny cuts in.

"Why don't we all go in November for Thanksgiving?" he suggests. "It'll be less crowded, and I can take some time off work."

I spot our aunt across the courtyard and gesture toward her, steering the conversation. I don't want to have this conversation. "There's Tía Lupe."

We weave through the crowd. "¡Hola, Tía!" Sara calls out, rushing forward to embrace her.

"¡Hola, mis niños!" Tía Lupe beams, noticing us.

We exchange hugs, and when her eyes meet mine, they soften, filled with an understanding that stirs something deep in my chest. It's a look I've grown to recognize—the look of quiet pity and careful kindness. The empathy look.

I hate it.

We spend some time catching up, talking about Tía Lupe's recent trip to Mexico but Sara's curiosity soon gets the better of her.

"Tía, que nos mandó mi abuela?" she asks eagerly.

With a smile, Tía Lupe pulls a black plastic bag from her tote. "Su abuela dice que no es mucho, pero lo manda con mucho amor. Y lo mandó a bendecir," she says as she hands it to Sara.

After making plans for dinner next Sunday, we exchange goodbyes and head home. Sara can barely contain her excitement. Manny and I agree to wait until after dinner to open the gifts, much to her dismay. To distract her, I let her pick what we'll watch while Manny takes over the kitchen.

The scent of garlic and onions soon fills the air, mingling with the quiet hum of the TV. Sara flips through channels with restless enthusiasm, unable to settle on anything. Her indecision becomes a soothing background rhythm, and I find myself sinking deeper into the couch cushions, my eyelids growing heavier.

Before I realize it, I'm dozing off.

The soft glow of moonlight filters through the curtains, casting a gentle light over the room. But suddenly, I'm no longer on the couch. I'm standing in a lush garden, surrounded by vibrant blooms and the thick scent of jasmine. A deep sense of peace washes over me. In the middle of the garden, I see my grandmother, her weathered hands cradling a flower as she examines it.

"Todos tenemos un ángel de la guardia que nos cuida," she says, her voice soft like a lullaby. "Por eso siempre tienes que portarte bien."

I'm drawn to her, her words pulling me closer like a magnet. But something shifts, subtle at first—an undercurrent of something darker, something wrong.

"Y si no me porto bien, qué pasa, abuela?" I ask, though the words feel distant, like they don't really belong to me.

She turns, her expression darkening. "Then I will come for you."

Her voice drops, sending a chill down my spine. The peaceful garden begins to warp, twisting around me as my grandmother's kind face twists, her skin melting away to reveal skeletal features beneath. Her eyes, once full of warmth, now gleam with something sinister. I'm frozen in place, my feet glued to the ground as the ghastly figure inches closer, a horrifying smile creeping across her bony face.

I try to scream, but the sound dies in my throat. The figure—no longer my grandmother—reaches out, her skeletal hand inching toward me. Panic surges through me as I squeeze my eyes shut, desperate to wake up, to end the nightmare and—

I jolt awake. Sara's hand rests gently on my shoulder, her face etched with concern. "Dinner's ready," she says, her voice pulling me out of the nightmare and back to the present.

My heart is still racing as I follow Sara to the kitchen table, the edges of the dream clinging to me, refusing to fade. We eat mostly in silence, Manny focused on his meal while Sara, too excited about what's coming next, barely says a word. After we finish, Manny finally pulls out the black plastic bag from where it sat beside him, sliding it across the table to Sara. Her eyes light up as she eagerly opens it, pulling out a few items—small religious bracelets made of knotted cord—and a letter from Grandma.

"These are for protection," Sara says, reading aloud. She hands me a black bracelet with a simple cross woven into the design.

I turn it over in my hands, feeling the rough texture of the knots. It's small and unadorned, almost fragile-looking, but when I slip it onto my wrist, it fits perfectly, the weight of it oddly comforting. The cross presses lightly against my skin with every movement, like it's meant to be there.

Grandma's superstitions always felt sweet, if a little old-fashioned, but now, something about this bracelet stirs an unexpected warmth in my chest. She believes these cords, blessed by prayer, can protect against unseen forces—against the shadows that linger in the corners of the world. *Gotta love Grandma.* My fingers trace the knots absently. It feels like a promise, a tether to something bigger than myself.

That night, as Sara brushes her teeth in the bathroom, I sit on the edge of my bed, absently running my fingers over the black bracelet on my wrist. The knots feel smooth and solid beneath my touch, grounding me. But the dream from earlier lingers, refusing to fade.

"Sara," I call out, my voice cutting through the quiet.

The rhythmic swish of her toothbrush against her teeth suddenly stops. A second later, she pokes her head out of the bathroom, toothbrush in hand. "Hmm?"

"Do you think we all have someone looking out for us?"

She rinses her mouth and steps into the room, drying her face with a towel. "I think so," she says thoughtfully. "Maybe it's angels. Maybe it's something else. But yeah, I think someone—or something—is watching over us."

Her answer lingers long after we settle into bed. I trace the knots of the bracelet absently, my mind drifting back to Julian's voice.

At the time, I told myself it was just grief. A trick of my imagination.

But now, I'm not so sure.

The dream, the bracelet, the voice—they feel connected somehow, like pieces of a puzzle I can't quite put together.

Beneath the questions, something darker stirs. Anger.

Anger at God, at the universe, at whoever decided Julian's time was up. Therapy, mass, whispered prayers— they dull it, but they don't erase it.

Why? The question echoes, hollow and unanswered. *Why him?*

I push the thought aside and whisper a silent prayer for peace.

But when sleep comes, peace does not.

CHAPTER 12

I'm standing in darkness—endless, oppressive darkness. Yet ahead of me, three figures glow softly, their light cutting through the void. I step closer, my breath hitching when I recognize one of them. Julian.

But he's not alone.

Beside him stand two other figures, so radiant they seem to be made of light itself.

The man closest to me radiates warmth, his glow gentle, softening the heavy air around him. His features are striking, as though sculpted from marble, with hazel eyes that hold a quiet compassion. His tousled chestnut hair frames a face that feels timeless—youthful yet ancient, mortal yet eternal. There's something steady about him, something calming, though I can't ignore the awe he inspires.

Beside him stands a woman, her presence no less striking. Her platinum-blonde hair flows like woven moonlight, every strand shimmering with an unearthly light. Her cerulean eyes are sharp and all-seeing, cutting through the darkness as though it bends to her will.

She stands tall, her posture regal, holding a wisdom far beyond human comprehension. Her glow is gentle but commanding, as though the light itself bends to her will.

"She's seen you. And now she's heard you," the man says, his voice calm but weighted with concern. "That's not normal."

"It was only once," Julian replies, a hint of defensiveness in his tone. "She hasn't seen or heard me since."

"But why you?" the woman asks, her piercing cerulean eyes narrowing. "She's never been able to hear any of us before. Ever."

Their words hang in the air, heavy and electric. What are they talking about? Me? Am I dreaming?

No, this feels more than just a dream. But if it's not a dream then where am I? Why is Julian here, with them?

"You shouldn't have intervened," the man says, his hazel eyes fixing on Julian. There's no anger in his voice, but his disapproval is clear.

"Julian," the woman begins, her voice calm but edged with authority. Her hair shimmers like liquid silver as she turns toward him, her glow pulsing faintly. "We understand this is still new to you. But there are rules— rules we are not allowed to break unless explicitly told otherwise. You overstepped."

"I couldn't just let her die." Julian's voice slices through the tension, steady and unflinching. "It wasn't her time. Isn't that what we're supposed to do? Protect?"

"It was her choice," the woman counters, her tone softening but losing none of its weight. Her eyes hold Julian's gaze, unyielding. "We tried. Again and again, we nudged her away from those thoughts and gave her every reason to stay. But she kept feeding into them. There's only so much we can do."

"It wasn't right," Julian begins, his voice rising with emotion. But before he can finish, I step forward, my own voice breaking through the tension.

"Julian, what's going on?" My words tremble, and so do I, as I inch closer. The oppressive shadows surrounding me retreat in the light of their glow, the warmth brushing against my skin.

The man's head snaps toward me, his hazel eyes widening in disbelief. The air around him ripples, like a stone cast into still water. "How is this possible?" he murmurs, his voice more to himself than anyone else.

"Chave, you—" Julian's voice falters, breaking as his eyes meet mine. He steps toward me, hesitant, his hand lifting as though to reach for me, but he stops short, his hand falling back to his side. "You're not supposed to be here."

It's only then that I notice their robes—white, luminous, and faintly shimmering with an inner light. The man and woman seem to tower over Julian, their presence almost unreal, filled with a quiet, unexplainable power. Yet, Julian stands with them, not diminished, but as their equal in this impossible trio.

The light from their robes spills into the surrounding darkness, casting them in a glow that makes them seem like living constellations. As though they belong to some other realm.

"She needs to go. Now," the woman says, her voice slicing through the stillness. Her eyes lock onto mine, and the force of her gaze is staggering. I feel her stare peeling back the layers of who I am, exposing pieces of me I didn't even know were there. A shiver races down my spine.

The glow surrounding them flickers, dimming as the darkness around us surges like a living thing. It rushes forward, swallowing the light in one violent surge.

The last thing I see is Julian's face—his lips parting as though to speak, his expression filled with longing.

I wake with a gasp, my chest heaving as though I've surfaced from deep water.

The room is still. Moonlight filters through the curtains, painting soft patterns on the ceiling. Beside me, Sara's steady breathing is the only sound, a reminder of the real world. But my mind is racing.

The dream clings to me, I'm unable to shake it off. It felt too real—*too* vivid—like I had wandered somewhere forbidden, somewhere I was never meant to see.

A chill creeps down my spine, and I instinctively reach for the bracelet on my wrist. The knots feel rough and solid beneath my fingers, an anchor in the disorienting quiet of the room.

But my pulse thrums, my heartbeat loud in the silence. The only thought that keeps crossing my mind is that whatever that was, it wasn't a dream.

And Julian ... What does he have to do with all of this?

CHAPTER 13

The dream from last night still has a grip on me, refusing to let go no matter how hard I try to shake it off. It feels like I've stumbled across a puzzle I was never meant to find, its missing pieces scattered all around me. And now, I can't stop myself from trying to put it together.

Julian's presence was too real, too vivid for it to be just a figment of my imagination.

And the man's words about "intervening," what did he mean? Was he talking about the day I tried to take my life? I remember the way Julian had shown up right before I lost consciousness. I had convinced myself it was nothing more than grief—a cruel trick of my mind, born out of guilt and desperation. But now ...

Now I'm not so sure.

Could it have been real?

And those other two—the angelic figures cloaked in light—where do they fit in? Who were they?

The questions swirl in my mind, drawing me deeper into a mystery I can't untangle. Every answer I reach for only leads to more questions, like wandering a maze with no end. It's maddening, and yet there's something about it that feels important. Like I'm standing on the edge of discovering something profound, something that's been waiting for me to understand.

I absentmindedly run my fingers over the bracelet on my wrist.

Just as I'm sinking further into my thoughts, a voice cuts through, soft yet unmistakable.

You know the answer.

"What?" I blurt out, startled.

Manny looks up from his plate, breaking the quiet. "I didn't say anything."

A nervous laugh escapes me. "Sorry, I thought I heard you say something."

He frowns, his brows knitting together as he tries to mask the worry in his eyes. "You sure you're okay?"

Normally, little things like this wouldn't raise an eyebrow. But I get it—why every strange thing I do feels like a red flag now. After what I tried to do, I can't blame him for being concerned.

I force a smile, trying to ease his worry. "Yeah, I'm fine. You should probably get started with work soon."

Manny still looks unsure, lingering for a moment longer, but he nods. Before he can say anything else, Sara walks into the kitchen, breaking the tension with her usual flair.

"Alrighty, hijos, I'm off. Manny, don't forget, it's your turn to cook tonight!" she teases, her voice bright as she grabs her bag.

Manny rolls his eyes, exasperated but amused. "Can you stop calling us *hijos?* I'm older than you, and I'm the one who actually parents around here."

"Uy, no te enojes," she says with a dramatic wave of her hand. "Nomas digo. Anyway, I'm out. Bye!"

Manny pushes back from the table, picking up his coffee mug. "I'll get to work," he says, his tone softer now. "Let me know if you need anything."

I nod absently, my thoughts already drifting back to the dream as he heads to the home office. I finish my breakfast quickly, rinse the dishes, and then settle onto the couch, switching on the TV.

But I can't focus.

There's a nagging feeling that is telling me to look for answers. The voice that I heard from earlier was unfamiliar, but I can't stop thinking about what it told me. That I already know the answer. But do I?

Then there's the voice I heard months ago that I'm sure was Julian's. Now I'm certain that it wasn't a hallucination.

Intrigued and uneasy, I grab my phone and start typing "guardian angels" into the search bar. I need answers.

To my surprise, dozens of articles pop up—everything from blogs to religious forums. I scroll through discussions on connecting with guardian angels, recognizing their signs, and personal stories of divine intervention. Apparently, people believe you can have more than one guardian angel.

The thought is comforting ... and unsettling.

One article catches my eye. It explains a common belief that a departed loved one can become a spiritual guide. My heart skips a beat as I read. Could Julian be my spirit guide? Could it be that the other two beings from my dream are my guardian angels?

But nowhere in the article does it mention being able to *hear* them. Signs, yes—dreams, symbols, feelings—but direct communication? That's rare, almost unheard of.

So why can I hear Julian? And if those other two are my guardian angels, then how is that I was able to see them and talk to them?

Growing up Catholic, I knew about guardian angels, but they always felt more like an abstract concept than actual beings. When I prayed, it was to God or the Virgin Mary, not to angels. My mom had taught us a prayer to our guardian angels when we were kids, but I only said it when I was scared—like when the shadows in my room took strange shapes or when I thought I heard voices in the night.

I never truly believed they were real.

But now? Now it feels like there's more to it than I ever allowed myself to imagine.

The idea of Julian becoming my spiritual guide stirs something strange inside me—a mix of comfort and confusion. It makes sense, in a way. He was always there for me, always watching out for me. But why is all this happening, now?

A dull ache begins to creep into my temples, the questions swirling in my mind pressing harder, refusing to leave me alone.

I close my eyes and press my fingers lightly against my forehead, as though I can rub away the tension. But the questions remain, the puzzle pieces just out of reach.

I feel it—like I'm on the verge of something, some truth hovering just beyond my grasp.

The weight of it pulls at me, dragging me down, and slowly, I let myself drift into sleep.

"Chave, run!"

Julian?

"Run!"

I blink and find myself standing in the middle of a dense forest. The trees loom tall and thick, their shadows swallowing everything in darkness. There's no sound—no wind, no rustling leaves, no distant wildlife. Only silence, eerie and suffocating. My heart pounds in my ears.

I see Julian a few feet ahead of me, his back toward me, like he's shielding me from something. There's an urgency in the air, a sense of looming danger, though I can't see it yet.

"I said run!"

Just as I'm about to ask what's happening, something emerges from the shadows—a figure. Tall, skeletal, with glowing red eyes that burn through the darkness. The stench hits me before the sight of it fully registers, an overwhelming, rotten odor that makes my stomach churn. My body tenses in fear, my legs frozen in place. I want to run, I want to scream, but my body won't respond. Every instinct in me screams *La Muerte*.

The skeletal figure moves closer, its glowing eyes locked on me. My throat tightens as I try to speak, to call out to Julian, but all I manage is a weak, trembling whisper.

"Julian ..."

"Chave, I love you," Julian says, his voice steady and filled with sorrow. "No matter what happens, remember that I love you. I'll always love you. And I won't let anything happen to you."

His words settle over me like a blanket of warmth, even as fear grips my chest. But something feels final about his tone—a goodbye wrapped in reassurance. Before I can call out again, the skeletal figure takes another step forward, its red eyes glowing brighter.

Boom!

I jolt awake, my heart racing, my body drenched in cold sweat. The sound of an explosion blares from the TV, some action scene from the show still playing, but I barely register it. My breath comes fast and shallow as I wipe my hands across my face, trying to shake off the lingering dread clinging to me like a shadow.

Another dream. But this one felt different ... darker.

I sit up slowly, rubbing my eyes with trembling hands. Something is coming. I can feel it—something bad. The ache in my chest grows taught, and my thoughts spiral, racing too fast to catch. Julian's words echo in my mind, *I won't let anything happen to you.*

But there was something final about the way he said it, like he was preparing me for whatever is coming. I shiver, my hand instinctively moving to the black bracelet on my wrist. The rough knots feel solid beneath my fingers, but there's no comfort in them now—only a sense of foreboding that sinks deeper into my bones.

Whatever this is, it's not over. Not by a long shot.

CHAPTER 14

"Have you been getting enough sleep?" my therapist asks, her tone gentle as always.

"Mostly," I reply, keeping my answer short. I don't want to dive into the truth behind my restless nights—the ones spent staring at the ceiling, chasing questions I can't answer.

She studies me for a moment, her eyes thoughtful but patient before continuing. "Good. How have you been doing with concentration and focus?"

I hesitate, choosing my words carefully. The truth is, my concentration has been consumed by things I can't fully explain—even to myself. How could Dr. Rivera begin to understand? She'd probably tell me I've found some new way of coping, another distraction from the grief.

"Um, I think it's normal," I say finally, trying to sound convincing.

She nods, making a note in her notepad. "Okay, good. You've been attending mass and spending time with your family. Do you feel like that's still helping?"

"Well ... yes," I answer. As I speak, the image of Julian standing with those two other beings flashes across my mind, vivid and unshakable. It reminds me of the one thing I can't admit to her. I'm trying to figure out if there's really something beyond death.

Ever since the idea struck me that Julian might be my spirit guide, I've been trying to reach out to him. I've prayed. I've meditated. I've begged for a sign, any sign. But there's been nothing—no flicker of communication, no sense of his presence. It feels like shouting into a void, and the silence leaves me more lost than ever.

But I can't say any of this to Dr. Rivera. What if she thinks I'm clinging to delusions? What if she sees it as a red flag, proof that I'm grasping at things that aren't there? It would raise alarms, and if Sara found out, she'd tell Manny. I can't even begin to imagine what would happen then.

"That's good," Dr. Rivera says, pulling me out of my thoughts. "I've been working with you for a little over three months now. We've been taking things at your pace, which is exactly what we needed to do. But I want to let you know that I think you're in a better spot now, and when you're ready, I'd like to start diving into the harder stuff."

She pauses, her gaze warm and understanding, like she's giving me the space to take her words in. "As I've told you from the beginning, this isn't easy work. It takes time, and there will be days that are harder than others. But I'll always respect your limits."

"Okay," I say quietly, the hesitation clear in my voice. I'm not sure what diving deeper entails, and the thought sends a ripple of unease through me. I'm afraid to ask, afraid to find out.

"We'll continue to meet twice a week, but eventually I would like to go to once a week."

"Okay," I reply.

When I step into the lobby, Sara's car is already waiting for me out front, right on time, as always. I can see her through the window, looking down at her phone. When I open the car door, she jumps slightly, startled.

"What are you looking at that has you so focused?" I ask, buckling my seatbelt.

"Uh … nothing," she says too quickly. I raise an eyebrow, but decide not to push it.

The drive home is quiet, the low hum of music filling the background. The words of the song are barely audible. As we pass the library, my eyes are drawn to the old brick building, its large windows glowing faintly in the late afternoon light.

Suddenly, I feel it—a strange pull, sharp and undeniable, like something unseen is urging me to go inside. It feels as though the building itself is calling out to me.

I lean forward in my seat. "Sara, can you pull into the library parking lot?"

"What?" she asks, glancing at me with a raised eyebrow.

"Just … please," I say, my gaze fixed on the building as an inexplicable sense of purpose wells up inside me.

I've already spent hours online, searching for answers about spirit guides, only to fall into endless rabbit holes of conflicting theories and half-formed ideas. Maybe the library will have something more.

Sara hesitates, then shrugs and turns into the lot. "This is random," she says, breaking the silence as she peers out the window. Her curiosity is obvious. "We haven't been to a library in forever."

As we get out of the car and walk toward the entrance, her expression flickers with interest. "What's up with this sudden library trip?"

I manage to give her a smile but don't say anything.

Stepping into the cool, hushed air of the library, the familiar scent of old books and polished wood wraps around me, bringing back a flood of memories I didn't realize I missed. Rows of bookshelves stretch out before us, filled with stories and knowledge waiting to be uncovered.

I used to love coming to the library. It was my safe haven, a place where I could disappear into other worlds. But as I got older, life got in the way, and I slowly stopped coming. I haven't picked up a book in over six years.

"It's been a while," I admit, my voice soft.

Sara raises an eyebrow. "Alright, spill. ¿Por qué el interés, si ya tienes años que no has leído?"

I manage a half-hearted smile. "Por eso. I think it's time I start picking up old hobbies again."

Her eyes widen in surprise, but she quickly masks it with a casual shrug. "Okay, I can get behind that. I'll get us set up with library cards."

I'm sure she thinks that I'm finally taking baby steps forward, that I'm trying to reconnect with myself. But that's far from the truth.

"Thanks," I say as she heads toward the help desk, smiling as though nothing is out of the ordinary.

While Sara talks to the librarian, I wander through the aisles, running my fingers along the spines of books, their titles blurring together as I pass. Then, a particular section catches my eye. Spirituality.

I walk toward it, my heartbeat quickening. My eyes skim through the rows of titles until one stops me in my tracks, *Connecting with Your Spirit Guides: A Beginner's Guide.* I pull the book from the shelf, feeling a flicker of anticipation. Maybe this will have the answers I've been looking for.

Settling into a cozy corner, I flip open the book and begin reading. Time blurs as I skim chapter after chapter, searching for something that will make sense of my dreams, of Julian's presence, of the strange pull I can't explain. So far, nothing new—nothing I haven't already read online. I'm starting to feel frustrated, but I keep going, hoping the next page will have something different.

"Wow, huh. Okay?" Sara's voice startles me, and I glance up to find her standing over me, she kneels down to peek at the title.

"It's just a beginner's guide to spirituality stuff," I say, hesitating slightly. "Thought it might be interesting."

She studies me for a moment, her expression curious. She doesn't ask any questions, just takes two library cards from her purse and hands me one.

"Well, look at us. We're official now."

"Thanks, Sara," I say, taking one of the cards and tucking it into my wallet.

"Ready to check out some books?" Sara asks, standing up and offering me a hand.

"Absolutely," I reply, taking her hand as she helps me up to my feet.

"Let's see what other treasures we can find in this place," Sara says with enthusiasm.

We spend the next hour wandering through the endless shelves, occasionally showing each other random finds. By the time we step back outside, the sky has shifted to deep twilight, painted in shades of indigo and gold. The warm evening air brushes against my skin as I check my phone, surprised by how much time has passed.

We're each carrying three books when I realize we've missed dinner completely. I can already picture Manny's hangry expression. It's not pretty.

As we approach the front door, I can feel his impatience radiating from inside the house. The moment we step in, Manny glances up from the couch, his expression a mix of relief and exasperation.

"Seriously?" he groans. "I thought you two got lost or something." His eyes flick to the books Sara and I are carrying.

"We, uh, made a quick stop at the library," Sara says, holding up her stack of books with a sheepish grin. "Kinda lost track of time."

Manny exhales, his irritation softening just a little. "Great. But next time, can you lose track of time after dinner? Tengo hambre."

"Takeout," I suggest quickly, eager to sidestep any brewing tension. "No cooking, no hassle, we can eat faster."

Sara nods. "Works for me. What do you want, Manny?"

"Anything, as long as it's quick," he mutters, already turning his attention back to the TV.

Once dinner arrives we eat in the living room, the air filled with the sound of crinkling takeout bags and the mingling of fried rice and orange chicken. We eat mostly in silence with Sara's occasional commentary on the show Manny is watching. I pick at my food, too distracted to enjoy it. I really want to go through the books I got.

After we clean up, I retreat to my room, balancing the three books in my arms as I shut the door softly behind me.

I sit cross-legged on my bed, spreading the books out in front of me. My eyes linger on the one furthest to the right. It's the heaviest among the three, its dark cover smooth and slightly worn under my fingers.

The Numbers of Heaven: Finding Meaning in Angelic Signs.

I trace the embossed letters. Slowly, I open the book, the spine creaking faintly as though it hasn't been opened in a long time.

The first few pages describe angelic numbers, sequences believed to be messages from divine beings. Numbers that aren't random but deliberate—patterns sent to guide, protect, or reassure. I skim passages about the meaning of common numbers:

111: A reminder that your thoughts are manifesting your reality. Focus on the positive.

222: Encouragement that you're on the right path. Trust the process.

333: A sign of alignment. The ascended masters are with you.

444: Protection and support. Your guardian angels are near.

555: Change is coming. Be prepared for a shift.

The descriptions are brief but strangely comforting. It's as if these sequences are proof that someone—or something—is paying attention, reminding us we're not as alone as we feel.

I pause, thinking back to moments when I'd noticed recurring numbers. Had I ever really paid attention?

The answer comes easily. No. I've never taken the time to notice things like that.

I flip to another section of the book, one detailing how to recognize when angels are trying to communicate. They often use numbers, yes, but also dreams, feathers, coins, even sudden feelings of warmth or calm. Signs can be subtle or bold, depending on what's needed to get your attention.

The book describes how, throughout history, angelic numbers have been regarded as divine breadcrumbs, pointing people toward clarity, guidance, or answers. They're meant to make you stop, to shift your perspective, to notice what you'd otherwise overlook.

I keep reading while the minutes slip away unnoticed. I don't know how long I've been reading. I went from sitting to leaning up against the headboard.

The words start blurring together as my eyes grow heavy. Before I know it, the book slips from my fingers, landing with a soft thud against the blanket.

The pull of sleep is too strong, and I surrender to it, the weight of the day—and the questions I can't answer— dragging me under.

CHAPTER 15

I find myself once again standing in darkness. It's the same place from last time—the endless void where I met Julian and the two other beings.

Their voices echo faintly in the distance. I start walking toward them, drawn by the sound. As I move closer, a faint glow begins to pierce through the dark, the voices growing louder with every step.

I stop just short of the light, lingering in the shadows, hidden but close enough to listen.

"There's a shift," the woman says. Her words are calm, measured, but there's tension coiled beneath them.

"What does that mean?" Julian asks, his brow furrowed with concern.

"We're not sure," the man replies, his tone thoughtful. "But this has never happened before."

"So what's changed?" Julian presses.

The woman hesitates. "We have a theory …" she starts, but her voice wavers, the sentence trailing into silence.

Then, abruptly, her head snaps toward me, her cerulean eyes piercing the darkness where I stand.

I freeze.

It's as if she can sense me—feel my presence before even seeing me. Her eyes burn like twin beacons, cutting through the shadows that surround me.

I hesitate, unsure whether to step forward or stay hidden. But it's too late—I've been caught. Her gaze doesn't falter, and I know there's no use pretending.

So I step out of the shadows.

"You're here again," the man says, his voice filled with disbelief. "How is this possible?"

"You need to go," the woman commands, her tone more forceful this time.

I try to speak, to ask them what they mean, but the words won't come.

The darkness surges around me, and before I can make sense of it, I'm jolted awake.

I sit up, my heart racing. The room is dim, the faint glow from the hallway slipping through the crack in the door.

Another dream. Another strange, inexplicable dream. But this one felt ... different.

I rub my temples, trying to piece it all together. This can't just be a dream. It doesn't feel like one. It's too vivid, too real—just like the others.

If I'm right, if these aren't just dreams, then… Julian.

Is he my spirit guide?

The thought sends a jolt through me, my pulse racing. *I can see him again.*

Somehow, I know I will. I don't know how—but I'll find a way.

Another thought crosses my mind. They were talking about a shift. I don't know what it means, but it feels important.

Why are they so concerned? It feels like I'm on the edge of something—something beyond my understanding.

An overwhelming feeling washes over me—a pull, like a thread tugging at my chest. I know what it's telling me, even though I've been avoiding it for so long.

I need to visit Julian's grave.

But the thought alone sends a wave of anxiety crashing through me. I haven't been back since the funeral. His family... they made it clear I wasn't welcome. The memory of their cold stares and whispered insults still burns in my mind. Even though Julian was my family too, even though he was my love, I don't think I can face them again. Not yet. Maybe not ever.

But maybe ... maybe I'm supposed to go. Maybe that's where I'll find the answers I need.

"Hey, you awake?" Sara's voice breaks through the haze of my thoughts as she peeks into our room.

"Yeah," I reply quietly, still trying to steady my breathing.

"You should probably change and wash your face. You'll feel better," she says, her voice light but caring.

I hesitate, then muster the courage to ask. "Sara, do you think you and Manny could come with me to visit Julian after church on Sunday?"

Her eyes widen, but she quickly hides her surprise. "¡Claro que sí!" She smiles gently, stepping into the room. "We'll be there with you."

A knot tightens in my chest, a mixture of fear and relief. I'm not ready for the weight of what's to come, but I know this is something I need to do. And having Sara and Manny by my side... maybe that will give me the strength to face it.

CHAPTER 16

As we make our way along the winding path of the cemetery, my hands start to become clammy. My heart pounds in my ears, a relentless drumbeat drowning out everything else. Up ahead, a car comes into view, and my breath catches in my throat. My head spins. Is it Julian's family?

Relief washes over me as unfamiliar faces climb into the car and drive away. I exhale a breath I hadn't realized I was holding.

Manny pulls the car to a stop. The engine cuts off. I take a few deep breaths before stepping out. We don't speak as we follow the narrow gravel path toward Julian's grave. The crunch of our footsteps being the only sound that follows us.

When Julian's tombstone comes into view, my hands begin to tremble. I clench them at my sides, but it does nothing to steady them. Sara notices my distress and gently takes my hand. Her grip is warm and comforting.

"Hey, cuñado," Sara says softly, kneeling to place flowers on Julian's grave. "Sorry it took us so long to bring you your wife. But you know how hard it's been for her, so you understand. Please keep looking after her."

Her words hit me like a blow, and I flinch. That last part—her request for Julian to keep watching over me—cuts too close. It feels as if she knows something. An urge rises inside me to confront her, to demand answers. But I shove it down. There's no way Sara would know what I've been experiencing lately.

Manny clears his throat, breaking the silence. "Sara and I will give you some space. Take your time," he says gently, guiding her away with a hand on her shoulder.

"Thank you," I murmur.

And then I'm alone with Julian. Alone with my thoughts. Alone with the crushing reality of Julian's absence. I take a deep breath and stare down at the tombstone, trying to gather the strength to speak.

I need to say something. Anything.

"Hey, Julian," I begin, my voice trembling. The words catch in my throat. This isn't the conversation I imagined having. "I—" I falter, unsure of how to continue. My heart feels like it's being torn in two.

"Thank you ... for saving me that day," I manage, my voice a thin whisper. "I'm sorry I wasn't strong enough. I'm sorry I couldn't ... I don't know how to live without you. We were supposed to do this together. Everything. All of it."

The tears come then, blurring my vision, the weight of my grief pressing down on me like an anchor. "I miss you with every fiber of my being, Julian. Time keeps passing, but the pain doesn't fade. I still feel so lost ... so completely lost without you."

The words spill out in a rush, unfiltered, raw. "I love you," I whisper, my voice breaking. "I love you so much."

For a moment, there's only silence. Then, faint but unmistakable, I hear it.

I love you too, Chave, mi amor.

"Julian?" I gasp, my eyes wide, frantically searching the space around me. There's no one. No sign of him. No trace. But I know I heard it. His voice. Clear as day.

"Julian?" I call out again, my voice rising, desperate. "Please ... I need you."

But there's nothing. Just the quiet rustle of the wind and the stillness of the cemetery. The silence presses down on me, and after ten long minutes of pleading into the void, I give up.

I drag myself back to the car, my heart heavy, my mind swirling in a chaotic storm. The ride home passes in a blur, each mile stretching endlessly before us. When we finally pull into the driveway, I don't wait for anyone. I stumble inside and retreat to my room, seeking refuge in the only place I can—the solitude of my bed.

Curling up into a ball, I pull my knees to my chest, squeezing tight, as if I can hold myself together with sheer force. My chest aches with the weight of everything—of

Julian, of my grief, of the overwhelming need to hear his voice again.

The dreams that once offered a flicker of hope now feel like cruel taunts, reminding me of something I can't have. And that voice ... the one I was so sure was real—it feels like it's slipping further away. A sinking feeling settles in my stomach as the truth sets in. This obsession, this desperate need to connect with him, has consumed me. It's become a prison, trapping me in my own grief, and I don't know how to break free.

Tears slip down my cheeks, hot and silent. I tighten my grip around myself, trying to hold on, but it's like the shattered pieces of my heart are slipping through my fingers, one by one.

Footsteps approach, soft and steady. The bed dips beside me, and then Sara's arms are around me, pulling me close. She doesn't speak, her embrace alone offers all the comfort I need. My sobs grow louder as I cling to her, finally letting the storm inside me break free.

A few moments later, I hear more footsteps, then a pause at the doorway. I know it's Manny. He doesn't say anything, but I feel the steadiness of his presence, his silent support. He retreats, giving me space, but the knowledge that he's there, that they're both here, is a small comfort.

The room falls into a pervasive silence, broken only by the sound of my sniffles as the sobs subside. Sara stays beside me, her warmth anchoring me, reminding me that I'm not alone.

After what feels like hours, I slowly sit up, wiping away the last of my tears. My breath still comes in shaky bursts, but the raw, sharp edge of my grief has dulled for the moment.

I glance at Sara, her eyes full of understanding. "Thank you," I whisper, my voice hoarse. "I don't know what I'd do without you."

Sara smiles gently, her hand resting on my shoulder. "You don't have to do this alone, Elle. We're here for you. Always."

Her words settle over me, and something inside me shifts. I've been so consumed by my grief, by the weight of Julian's absence, that I've failed to see the support that's been here all along. Manny and Sara—they've been quietly holding me up, never pushing, never forcing me to move on before I'm ready. They've given me space to grieve, to process, but they've never left me to do it alone.

It's because of them that I've been able to step away from work and take the time I need. Manny and Sara have helped cover the mortgage. And I still have the savings Julian and I built as well as the money I received from his life insurance. It's enough for me to take off more than a year if I wanted to or at least until I can figure out how to rebuild my life. The realization is humbling, and for the first time in weeks, a flicker of gratitude sparks within me.

But even as I acknowledge their presence, I know the dreams of Julian, the voice I heard today, can't be my anchor anymore. Whether it was real or not, I can't live in the past, waiting for something that may never come. Julian is gone. That's the truth I have to face, no matter how much it hurts.

The ache in my chest clenches, and for a moment, the tears threaten to spill again. But I push them back. I need to keep going. I need to live. For myself. And for him. He would have wanted me to.

As hard as it is—and as hard as it will continue to be—I have to start trying. Trying to figure out how to move forward, how to live this life without Julian in it. I owe it to him to keep living. To find some way, somehow, to pick up the pieces and rebuild.

CHAPTER 17

"How has this last week been for you?" Dr. Rivera asks as we settle into the session.

"It's been … rough." I admit remembering my breakdown I had two days ago after visiting Julian's grave.

"Can you tell me more about it? What made it rough?" she asks.

"I visited Julian's grave …" I start but pause, debating whether I should tell her about my dreams.

I've convinced myself the dreams are just another way my mind is trying to cope with the grief—nothing more. I start telling Dr. Rivera about the strange dreams, minus the voices I've heard.

She listens attentively, her pen moving across the notebook in her lap, the faint scratch of it filling the silence.

"Visiting his grave must have brought up a lot of emotions," she says, setting her pen down and giving me her full attention. "What were you feeling in that moment?"

I glance down at my hands, twisting my wedding ring around my finger.

"I don't know … everything, I guess. Guilt. Sadness. Anger. It's hard to explain. It just—" I stop, struggling to find the words. "It just hit me all at once, like a wave I couldn't stop."

She nods, her expression calm and understanding. "And the dreams you mentioned—do they happen often?"

"Lately, yeah." I hesitate. "I was having them almost every night, except for the past couple of nights."

Dr. Rivera tilts her head slightly, her gaze soft. "What do you think has changed over the past couple of nights? Why do you think the dreams have stopped?"

"I don't know," I say truthfully.

I don't know why I stopped dreaming. If I dream, I don't remember it.

She studies me for a moment, her expression thoughtful. Then, she asks, "Elle, we've talked about the grief cycle, and we know that everyone moves through it differently. But I haven't asked you yet—what is grief to you?"

The question catches me off guard. *Grief? What is grief to me?*

I look down again, my fingers still working the wedding ring. The silence stretches between us, but she doesn't rush me.

Finally, I speak, my voice quiet but steady. "It's … suffocating. Some days, it feels like I'm drowning—like I can't come up for air, no matter how hard I try. And other days …" I pause, searching for the right words. "Other days, it feels calm, like the water's finally still, and I can breathe again. But it never really goes away."

I stop twisting the ring and let my hands fall into my lap, staring at them as if the answer is written there. "It's always there, in the background. Even when it's quiet, I can feel it. Like I'm carrying it with me wherever I go."

Dr. Rivera nods slowly, her expression gentle. "That's a powerful description, Elle. It sounds like your grief is something that's always present, but its weight changes from day to day. Would you say that feels true for you?"

I nod, swallowing hard. "Yeah. It's like … I've learned how to live with it, but I'm never really free of it. Not completely."

Dr. Rivera is quiet for a moment, then asks, "When Julian appears in your dreams, does the weight of your grief feel different? Heavier or lighter?"

The question makes something twist inside me, and I hesitate. I hadn't thought about it that way before. "Lighter," I whisper after a moment. "But also … harder. I can see him and talk to him without touching him. It makes me feel like he's not really gone. But when I wake up …" I trail off, the knot in my throat tightening until I can't speak.

She nods, "Waking up brings the weight back. That makes sense. Grief is complicated—it doesn't stay in one place. Sometimes our dreams give us what we're longing for, even if it makes reality harder when we wake. Have you thought about what Julian's presence in your dreams might mean for you?"

Before I can respond, she continues. "Grief can also feel lonely. Like a companion you never asked for, one that isolates you from others, even the people who want to help."

I blink, the word hitting me harder than I expect. "Lonely," I repeat softly, testing it out.

She nods. "It's something many people feel in grief. But it's not just isolation—grief can also change us. It can shift the way we see the world, the way we remember the people we've lost. How do you think your grief has changed you?"

Her words stir something I've been avoiding. Emily.

I think of her unanswered calls, the messages I keep ignoring. She still reaches out, still tries. But I can't bring myself to let her in. Not yet. I tell myself it's because I don't know how to be around her anymore—around any of my friends. I barely know how to be around my own family outside of Sara and Manny.

I just don't know how to exist in a friendship that once included Julian. But maybe it's more than that. Maybe grief has made me selfish, wrapping me so tightly in my own pain that I can't see past it.

I swallow hard, my gaze dropping to my hands. "Yeah," I murmur. "I know what you mean."

I twist my wedding ring, staring down at it, unsure if I even want to say more. My eyes flick to the clock. 5:55 p.m.

I only have five more minutes.

Then it hits me. 555.

What did that book say 555 meant? Change. Change is coming.

I push the thought away. It's just a coincidence.

"We'll stop here for today," Dr. Rivera says, breaking through my thoughts. "I'll see you on Thursday?"

"Yes, Thursday," I reply, standing.

I thank her before heading out. In the lobby, I spot Sara waiting just outside, scrolling through her phone.

Stepping into the warm evening air, I slide into the car. She glances up. "¿Todo bien?"

I nod, forcing a small smile. "Yeah, I'm fine."

It's a lie, and I think she knows it. But she doesn't push. Instead, she starts the car, and we drive home in silence, the faint hum of music filling the space between us.

I stare out the window, my mind replaying Dr. Rivera's question. *How has grief changed me?*

I've lost myself. I don't know who I am anymore. I don't recognize the person staring back at me in the mirror. Grief changed everything.

I look over at Sara, her face illuminated by the evening rays of sunlight. She doesn't notice me watching her, but for a moment, I feel a pang of gratitude that she's here, even if I can't bring myself to talk about everything.

When we pull into the driveway, I hesitate before getting out of the car. There's a strange heaviness in the air, something I can't quite put my finger on. *Something feels ... off.*

But I shake it off. It's probably just my imagination. I follow Sara inside, the door clicking shut behind me. A shiver runs down my spine, though the house isn't that cold. It's that same creeping sensation I've felt before, like I'm being watched, like I'm not alone.

I step into the dimly lit hallway, the shadows stretching long and quiet. The air feels dense, charged with something unseen, something waiting.

Then—Julian.

His face flickers in my mind, so clear it makes me pause. His warm eyes, his familiar presence—it's as if he's there, just beyond my reach. Watching. Protecting. Keeping me safe.

A shiver snakes down my spine.

And then, just as quickly as he appeared—something else stirs.

A whisper.

Faint. Wrong. Too close.

It coils at the edges of the silence, just beyond what I can hear, what I can *see*.

The air thickens, pressing against my skin. I can't tell if it's grown colder—or if *something* is drawing nearer.

I squeeze my eyes shut and shake my head. *It's nothing.*

And yet, I swear the shadows move when I turn away.

CHAPTER 18

Several days have passed since our visit to the cemetery. As I promised myself, I've slowly begun easing back into the rhythm of life, contributing to the house chores that Manny and Sara have shouldered for so long. They were surprised when they caught me putting dishes in the dishwasher. Sara tried to take over, but I stood my ground—this was something I needed to do. I won that small battle, making it clear I was determined to start pulling my weight again. Dinner, however, remains the one exception. My siblings don't trust my cooking.

Tonight, it's Sara's turn in the kitchen. I offer to help, but she waves me away, insisting she can manage. So, I settle on the couch, mindlessly scrolling through shows, not really paying attention. The sounds of Sara moving pots and pans around blend with the noise from the TV, forming a soft, indistinct hum that fades as I drift away.

Before I know it, I'm no longer on the couch. I'm in a dark forest, similar to the one where I encountered La Muerte. This time, the darkness is less suffocating, but the eerie silence remains, like the trees are holding their breath.

I search for Julian, my heart racing, but I'm utterly alone.

Suddenly, I hear rustling—first from my left, then from my right. I whip around, looking, but there's nothing. Just shadows.

"Julian?" I call out, my voice echoing through the trees.

Nothing. The silence presses in, amplifying the sound of my heartbeat. The air feels heavy with anticipation, as if something is waiting, watching.

Then, a voice—raspy, hollow—whispers my name. "Isabella."

I freeze, my blood turning to ice. I try to run, but my legs are rooted in place, immobilized by fear.

"Isabella," the voice calls again, closer this time, slithering through the darkness.

A figure steps forward, emerging from the shadows—a grin stretching across its face, eyes gleaming with an unnatural, menacing light. Fear surges in me, tightening its grip around my chest.

"Who are you?" I stammer, my voice barely a whisper.

The figure steps closer, the scent of decay filling the air between us. "Ay, Isabella. You know who I am," it replies, its grin widening, the voice disturbingly familiar.

That's when it hits me. *La Muerte*—the same entity from my last dream.

"I-I don't want anything to do with you," I manage, forcing the words out even though my voice trembles.

La Muerte chuckles darkly. "But you called for me, Isabella. You asked for help, remember?"

Confusion floods me. *Called for help? When?* I try to think back, but my mind is a blur. I never asked for this. I never summoned this thing. Did I?

"No ... I never called for you," I insist, trying to muster courage.

Its grin widens, the shadows around us thickening as it steps closer. "Oh, but you did. And now I've come to collect what's mine."

A cold ripple of desperation washes over me. I struggle, my limbs still paralyzed. I need to wake up—I need to get out of this nightmare. With every ounce of strength I can summon, I remind myself that this isn't real. *This is just a dream.*

"Julian, help me!" I cry out, my voice breaking.

For a moment, there's only silence, but then—a faint voice in the distance. "Isabella! Isabella, wake up!"

Julian's voice. It's him. I focus on it, like a lifeline in the darkness.

"I know you're scared," his voice comes again, stronger now, full of warmth. "But you can do this. You're stronger than you think. Now wake up!"

His words give me the strength to push back against the grip of the dream. Slowly, the dark forest begins to blur and fade, the heavy paralysis loosening its hold on me. The rustling, the rasping voice—all of it begins to fade into nothing.

With a sharp gasp, I jolt awake.

The first thing I register is the dim glow of the television, the flickering light casting soft shadows across the room. My breath is ragged, my heart hammering against my chest.

Then—movement.

I turn my head, my vision adjusting, and see Manny standing to the right of me, his brows knit together in concern. "Elle?" His voice is gentle but firm, pulling me back fully to the present. "You okay? You were tossing and turning like crazy."

The sounds of reality settle around me—Sara rustling in the kitchen, the low hum of the TV. I'm on the couch. I'm home. I'm safe.

But my body is still trembling, my hands shaking as if the nightmare hasn't fully let me go.

I swallow hard, trying to steady my breathing. "Yeah ... just a bad dream. I'm fine."

I get up from the couch, trying to shake off the lingering fear, but my legs feel weak, my heart still racing.

"When did you get home?" I ask, hoping to distract him from pressing further about the dream.

"Just now. You sure you're okay? You're shaking," Manny says, surprising me by taking my hands in his. His warmth slowly seeps into me, easing the cold panic still lingering in my bones.

I force a small smile. "I'm fine. It was just intense. A really scary nightmare."

He doesn't look entirely convinced, but he nods. "Okay, well ... dinner's ready. Let's eat. Sara made something that smells amazing."

As he turns toward the kitchen, I reach for my wrist, my fingers brushing against the black bracelet. For a moment, I wonder if it had done its job. If it had helped pull me out of that nightmare.

"You know," I say, following Manny toward the kitchen, "if you need to start going back into the office more, you can. Even if it's just half days. That way, Sara doesn't have to keep rearranging her schedule when you have meetings. I'm doing a lot better—I promise I can handle being alone for a few hours."

Manny glances back at me, his face relaxing slightly. "We'll see. I'll talk to Sara."

At dinner, Manny brings up the annual company dinner his job is hosting. It's his first one since he started working there, and he asks if we want to join him.

Sara immediately agrees, her excitement contagious. I hesitate.

It would be my first big event since Julian passed. Just the thought of it makes my stomach twist. The idea of being surrounded by people, of putting on a brave face ... it feels overwhelming.

But I know if I decline, Manny and Sara won't go either.

"Okay," I say, trying to ignore the flutter of anxiety in my chest. "I'll come."

Sara smiles, clearly relieved by my response. "It'll be fun. And we'll be with you the whole time."

As we finish dinner, I reflect on my decision. It's another step—a small one, but a step nonetheless. As hard as it is, I promised myself I'd start moving forward, even if it's in baby steps. And I intend to keep that promise.

CHAPTER 19

The day I've been dreading is finally here. Standing in front of the mirror, I adjust my dress, trying to steady the nervous knot tightening in my stomach. The reflection staring back at me feels unfamiliar, like a version of myself I haven't seen in ages. I smooth the fabric of my dress, take a deep breath, and head downstairs to meet my siblings.

As I reach the bottom of the stairs, I pause, taking them in. Manny and Sara look effortlessly put together, dressed in their finest. Manny's tall frame and sharp features give him an effortlessly polished look, his sleek suit only adding to his quiet confidence. Sara, in an elegant dress, moves with natural grace. Her wavy hair cascades over her shoulders, and there's an ease about her—like she was made for events like this.

I've always felt a little out of place next to them. Growing up, I used to joke that I was adopted because I looked so different from them—my darker, honey-colored complexion, petite frame, and straight dark hair always made me feel like the odd one out. Manny is over six feet tall, and Sara stands at 5'5" with perfect proportions, while I'm just 5'3" and still waiting for the kind of presence they both carry so naturally. The only thing that ties us together is our straight, raised nose that we inherited from Dad.

Looking at them now, I feel a familiar wave of self-consciousness, but there's something else, too. For the first time, I truly see how much they've changed. How much we've changed. I've been consumed by my own grief, that I didn't notice the sacrifices they've made for me.

Manny, now in his mid-thirties, put his own life on hold to help me through my darkest moments. He was in the middle of something promising—a relationship he barely talks about anymore—when my world fell apart. He didn't hesitate to be there for me, even though it meant sacrificing his own happiness.

And Sara—always so composed—has been hiding her own heartbreak. She went through a painful breakup while I was too wrapped up in my sorrow to even notice. How did I miss that? How did I let their lives fade into the background while I drowned in my own?

"Wow, que guapa mi hermanita!" Sara's voice snaps me out of my thoughts. There's genuine admiration in her eyes, and for a moment, the insecurities that cling to me like a second skin fade. Manny nods in agreement, offering a reassuring smile.

"Thanks," I murmur, feeling awkward but a little lighter.

"Ready?" Manny asks, his hand gesturing toward the door. It feels like an invitation not just to leave the house, but to leave behind some of the heaviness we've all been carrying.

With a deep breath, I nod, grateful for their support, even if I haven't been able to fully appreciate it until now.

The drive to the venue is filled with light chatter. Manny and Sara keep the conversation going, their voices blending with the soft hum of the car engine. I chime in occasionally, but mostly I listen, grateful for the distraction from the anxieties swirling in my chest.

Before I know it, we're pulling up to the hotel. Stepping out of the car, I take a deep breath, the warm night air brushing against my skin. We make our way inside, and as we enter the ballroom, the atmosphere changes immediately. The air buzzes of anticipation. Laughter, clinking glasses, and animated conversations fill the space. Crystal chandeliers cast a warm glow over the room, their light dancing off the elegantly dressed guests. It's beautiful—overwhelming, but beautiful.

Manny leads us to a table near the stage, where we're introduced to some of his colleagues. They're friendly, which eases some of my nerves, but I can still feel the pressure of everything—the grandeur of the room, the excitement in the air—it pushes down on me, reminding me how different life feels now.

Sara leans in, her eyes sparkling. "This place is incredible! I can't wait to see what the night has in store for us."

Her enthusiasm is contagious, and I find myself smiling back at her. For the first time, I realize that agreeing to come tonight wasn't just about being there for Manny—it was about me too. I've been so wrapped up in my grief, in the heaviness of loss, that I haven't let myself experience moments like this. Being here feels like a step toward something lighter.

I straighten in my seat, glancing at Manny, who's looking around the room with a satisfied smile. "Thank you for inviting us," I say softly. "I needed this."

Manny looks at me, his face tender. "I'm really glad you're here, Elle. Tonight's about making new memories. No worries. No heaviness. Just fun, okay?"

I nod, appreciating the sentiment. But as I look around the room, I can't help but feel a pang of sadness. Julian would've loved this. He would've soaked in the music, the food, the energy. A part of me still aches for those moments we won't ever get to share. But I remind myself—this is about living, about honoring his memory by finding my own way forward.

The CEO takes the stage after dinner, giving a speech about the company's achievements and future goals. As I listen, I can't help but think about how Julian would have been fascinated by this. His mind was always geared toward growth, ambition, and creating something meaningful. The thought of him here, sitting next to me, listening to the speech with that sparkle of excitement in his eyes, tugs at my heart.

But instead of sinking into the familiar abyss of loss, I take a deep breath and let the thought pass, like a gentle wave rolling in and out. He's not here. And as much as it hurts, that's the reality I have to accept.

When the speech ends, the lights dim, and the band begins playing a soft, melodic tune. Couples make their way to the dance floor, swaying to the music.

Sara nudges me with a playful grin. "Want to dance?"

I hesitate, but before I can answer, Manny jumps in. He extends his hand toward me, a twinkle in his eye. "May I have this dance, hermanita?"

His grin is infectious, and I can't help but smile. "Okay, sure."

He leads me to the dance floor, and as we move to the rhythm of the music, something inside me loosens. With each step, a little piece of the burden I've been carrying begins to fall away. The music swirls around us, and for the first time in a while, I let myself enjoy the moment.

Manny twirls me, and I let out a laugh—a sound that feels both unfamiliar and comforting. It's like finding a part of myself I thought was lost. The part that can still feel joy, despite everything.

As we dance, I glance down at the black bracelet on my wrist. I'm not sure if it's tied to the strange things I've been experiencing, but it feels like a quiet reminder that I'm safe here, in this moment.

When the song ends, Manny pulls me into a hug. "It's good to hear you laugh again," he says softly.

I smile, warmth spreading through me. "It feels good."

Back at the table, I catch Sara watching us, her eyes full of happiness. That's when I realize how much my healing matters to them, too. They've been waiting—patiently, lovingly—for me to return, even in small steps.

As the night winds down, we step outside to get some air. The stars above sparkle against the dark sky, and for the first time in what feels like forever, I feel a small sense of hope stir within me.

"I'm glad you came," Manny says softly, his voice carrying warmth.

"Me too," I reply, glancing at Sara, who's smiling at both of us. It's just a small moment, but it feels monumental.

Maybe this is what moving forward looks like—not in leaps, but in tiny steps.

The warm night air fills my lungs, and I close my eyes for a second, savoring the quiet. I'm not ready to let go of the past, but I finally realize I can start making room for new moments of joy. Julian will always be a part of me, but I know I have to keep moving forward.

Sara nudges me playfully. "Want to go back inside for one last dance?" she asks, her eyes full of mischief.

I hesitate. The night has been emotionally draining, but there's also a part of me that feels like I could handle one more song, one more shared moment. I glance at Manny, who grins and shrugs. "Why not?"

"Okay," I say, smiling as we turn to head back inside. "One last dance."

CHAPTER 20

The moment we step back into the ballroom, the atmosphere hums with energy. The band plays an upbeat tune, couples twirl across the floor, and laughter echoes through the grand room. Everything looks the same as when we stepped outside, but something in me feels slightly off—like a chord that's just a little off-key.

Returning to our table, I take a sip of my drink, the cool liquid refreshing as it slides down my throat. It has a strange, bitter aftertaste that I hadn't noticed before. I brush it off, thinking maybe the ice melted too much, but a faint unease lingers. Manny and Sara are soon back on the dance floor, lost in their rhythm, leaving me alone with my thoughts. I lean back, watching them glide beneath the chandeliers, and for a brief moment, I feel a sense of calm. It's the first time in months that I've felt connected to myself again, like some piece of the old me has resurfaced.

I close my eyes, letting the music wash over me. The steady thrum of the bass is almost hypnotic, but when I open my eyes again, the room tilts slightly, just enough to make me blink twice.

At first, it's barely noticeable—just a faint dizziness. I tell myself it's probably exhaustion. The night has been emotionally charged, after all. But the feeling intensifies. My vision blurs at the edges, like a slow-creeping fog clouding my thoughts. Another sip of my drink doesn't help—it only seems to deepen the unsettling sensation.

I scan the room, trying to find something steady to focus on, when a man approaches my table. He's tall, well-dressed, with dark hair slicked back in a way that seems too polished for this setting. His suit, sharp and flawless, fits him like it was tailored for this exact moment. His eyes latch onto mine with an intensity that feels immediately intrusive.

"Mind if I join you?" he asks, his voice smooth but with an edge I can't quite place.

I hesitate but nod, thinking a little conversation might help me shake this strange sensation. "Sure."

At first, his small talk is harmless—questions about the party, about the music—but his gaze never leaves my face, and the longer he talks, the more claustrophobic it feels. I smile politely, nodding where appropriate, but my discomfort grows with every lingering glance, every too-casual question.

He leans in closer, his cologne overwhelming, filling the small space between us. "You don't look like you're having much fun. Maybe I can change that?"

I force a laugh, trying to maintain the façade of politeness. "I'm fine, just tired."

"Tired?" he echoes, his voice dipping lower, the smile on his lips not reaching his eyes. "You sure that's all?"

Something about his tone makes my skin prickle. I sit up straighter, the room still swaying slightly as I reach for my drink. The cold glass feels like an anchor, something solid to hold onto, but as I take another sip, the bitterness stings sharper than before.

I realize, too late, that it's not exhaustion making me feel this way.

It's the drink.

I glance at the man again, his smile widening as if he's watching some private joke unfold. My pulse quickens, and I scan the room for a way out. The restroom sign catches my eye—a quiet haven away from this. Away from him.

"I need to step out for a moment," I murmur, standing quickly, too quickly. The world tilts violently, and I have to grip the edge of the table to steady myself.

"Are you okay?" he asks, but there's no real concern in his voice. Only amusement. Like he's enjoying this— enjoying me unraveling in front of him.

"I'm fine," I lie, forcing a weak smile before making my way toward the restroom, my steps unsteady. The dizziness washes over me in waves now, stronger with each step. My vision darkens at the edges, narrowing into a tunnel, and I have to steady myself against the wall.

Footsteps sound behind me. I don't have to turn to know it's him. The heavy sense of his presence is unmistakable. I quicken my pace, stumbling through the restroom door and into the harsh, sterile light. The cool tiles underfoot are a stark contrast to the suffocating warmth of the ballroom, but even the brightness doesn't clear my head.

I splash cold water on my face, hoping to snap out of this haze, but it barely helps. My heart pounds in my ears, louder than the music outside. Behind me, the door creaks open. I freeze, gripping the edge of the sink as dread settles deep in my stomach.

He's followed me.

I turn slowly, my breath catching in my throat as he steps inside, his expression unreadable but his intentions unmistakable. He locks eyes with me, his predatory grin widening.

"Looks like you need some help after all," he says, voice filled with sickening satisfaction.

Panic surges through me, tightening my chest as my legs threaten to give out. I step back, but he moves closer, cutting off the only exit. My vision swims, and I can barely make out his form now, just a dark silhouette against the too-bright lights. I try to scream, but no sound comes. My throat feels like it's closing, strangling the air inside me.

He grabs my arm, his grip like iron, pulling me toward him. I struggle weakly, but my limbs feel like they're moving through quicksand. The world tilts again, and the edges of my vision blur. His laughter fills the small space, cold and hollow, reverberating off the tiled walls.

Then, through the haze, I see him.

Julian.

He stands in the doorway, bathed in a soft, almost ethereal light. For a moment, I think I'm hallucinating, that the fear has conjured him from some desperate corner of my mind. But then he speaks, his voice clear and steady.

"Let her go."

The man's grip loosens slightly, and he turns to face Julian, his bravado faltering. "Who the hell are you?" he demands, his voice no longer confident.

Julian steps forward, his presence filling the room with a quiet, controlled intensity. "I'm someone you don't want to cross."

Something about Julian—his calm authority, the way he holds the man's gaze without blinking—shakes the man. He hesitates, his grip on my arm loosening completely.

"This isn't worth it," the man mutters, releasing me as if I've suddenly become too much trouble. He takes a step back, but Julian doesn't move, blocking his path to the door.

For a tense moment, the man hesitates, eyes darting between Julian and the door. Then, with a sharp breath, he skirts around him, keeping as much distance as possible before bolting through the door.

I collapse, my legs giving out beneath me, but Julian is there in an instant, catching me before I hit the ground.

His arms wrap around me, steadying me with a warmth that feels too real to be a dream.

"Chave, it's okay. I've got you," he says softly, his voice full of concern and something deeper—something I can't quite place.

Tears well up in my eyes, a mix of relief and fear still clinging to me. "Julian … how …?" I sputter, barely able to form the words.

"Don't worry about that now," he replies gently. "We need to get you out of here."

With one arm around me, Julian helps me to my feet. My legs are shaky, barely able to support my weight, but his presence keeps me steady. We move quickly through the hallway, away from the noise of the ballroom, the soft glow of the corridor lights offering a strange sense of calm after the chaos.

Finally, we find a chair tucked away in a quiet corner, away from the bustle of the main event. Julian eases me into a chair, crouching beside me, his hands still holding mine. The warmth of his touch is the only thing anchoring me to reality.

"Just breathe, Chave. You're safe now," he says, his voice soothing.

But even as his words sink in, I can't shake the overwhelming weakness that still lingers in my limbs. My vision blurs again, and I feel myself slipping toward unconsciousness. "Thank you, Julian," I whisper, my voice barely audible.

"Chave, listen to me. You're not okay." His voice grows more urgent. "I can't stay long. Where's your phone?"

Confused, I fumble for my phone, handing it to him with trembling hands. He scrolls quickly, his expression tense.

"Hi, Manny," Julian says into the phone, his voice tight with urgency. "Chave's been drugged. I need you to come right now."

The room spins faster, the world closing in around me. Julian's voice fades into the background as darkness swallows me whole.

CHAPTER 21

When I regain consciousness, the soft glow of a lamp casts gentle shadows across the room. The faint scent of lavender lingers in the air, meant to be calming, but it does little to ease the pounding in my head. I sit up slowly, the rustle of the blankets seeming unnervingly loud in the stillness.

As my eyes adjust, familiar surroundings take shape— the armchair in the corner, the abstract painting by the window. Home. I should feel safe here, but I don't. The events of the night press down on me like an incoming storm. My mind flashes back to the dark, spinning restroom ... the dizziness ... strong hands pulling me out ... a familiar face.

Julian.

A soft knock pulls me from the memory, and my pulse quickens. For just a moment, I wonder if it could be him—if it's even possible. But it's Manny who steps into the room, his face tight with concern and something else ... guilt.

"Hey, Elle," he says gently. "How are you feeling?"

"I'm ..." The words get stuck in my throat. I take a breath and force myself to meet his eyes. "I think I'm okay."

Manny crosses the room and sits beside me on the bed, placing his hand on my shoulder. His warmth should be reassuring, but the tension rolling off him is impossible to ignore.

"Estábamos muy preocupados por ti," he says softly. "Do you remember anything?"

I close my eyes, trying to grasp the scattered fragments of the night. The man who tried to hurt me ... the dizziness ... and then Julian—how could it be real? It feels like a fever dream, something I can't fully understand or trust.

"I remember some things," I murmur, my voice unsteady. "But it's blurry."

Manny listens quietly as I recount what I can—bits and pieces that feel distant and unreal. His grip on the blanket tightens with each word. But I can't bring myself to mention Julian. How could I? How do you tell someone that the person who saved you is someone who's supposed to be dead?

"Julian called me," Manny says suddenly, his voice dropping. "He told me you'd been drugged and needed help. At first, I thought it was a joke—but his voice... I knew it was him. And the fear in it..." He exhales sharply. "That's when I knew it was real. I got there as fast as I could."

My heart leaps in my chest, and suddenly the room feels too small. Julian called him? That means it wasn't just a dream. He was really there. My thoughts race, trying to make sense of the impossible.

"Did you see him?" I ask, my voice trembling. I need to know. I need to understand.

Manny runs a hand over his face, exhaustion clear in the slump of his shoulders. "No. By the time I got there, you were unconscious. No sé cómo es posible ..." His voice trails off, like he's trying to wrap his mind around it, same as me.

A sense of unease settles in, thick with unanswered questions. Julian was there. He pulled me from danger. I felt him. I know I did. But how?

"Manny ..." I begin, but my voice falters. Should I tell him everything? About the dreams and the times I've heard Julian before? My chest clenches. I don't even understand it myself. Before I can decide, another knock sounds at the door.

Manny's head jerks up. "Come in," he calls.

Sara rushes in, her eyes wide with worry. "Elle!" she breathes, relief flooding her voice. "¡Gracias a Dios!"

She's at my side in an instant, her hands hesitating midair, as if unsure where to offer comfort first. Her presence should be reassuring, but instead, it's a reminder of just how fragile everything feels.

"I'm fine," I say softly, managing a weak smile. "Just trying to make sense of it all."

Sara glances at Manny, and they exchange a look I can't quite read. Then she turns back to me, her expression still clouded with concern.

"Manny told me … about Julian," she says slowly, her voice hesitant.

I nod, the memory of his presence still swirling in my mind. "He was there. Right?"

Sara bites her lip, uncertainty flickering in her eyes. "Manny told me he called, but … yo no lo vi. I didn't see him."

The room feels like it's closing in again. "I remember him pulling me out of the restroom," I whisper, staring down at the blanket. "But after that … everything is hazy."

Manny leans forward, his brow furrowed. "Elle, that's not possible. Julian is gone. Are you sure it was him?"

There's something in his voice—like he's trying to convince himself, too.

My breath catches. I know what he means—it shouldn't be possible. But I felt him. I felt his hands on me, his presence. It wasn't a dream. It wasn't a hallucination.

"I don't know," I finally say, my voice shaking. "It's all a blur."

Manny sighs, rubbing the back of his neck. "First thing in the morning, we'll go to the doctor. Then we'll file a report. I thought getting you out of the house would help, and now this …"

I see the guilt in his eyes, the way it hangs over him like a shadow. Manny always takes the weight of the world on his shoulders.

I reach out and hug him tightly. "It's not your fault," I say firmly, pulling back to meet his gaze. "Please don't blame yourself."

He holds me close for a moment longer, but I can still feel the guilt lingering in the way his arms tense around me. When I pull away, I squeeze his hands.

"You did everything you could. I'm just glad you were there."

Manny nods, but his worry remains, etched in the lines of his face. "We'll figure it out, Elle. We can't just let this go."

Sara reaches over and squeezes my hand. "We'll get to the bottom of it. You're not alone in this."

"I know," I reply, though exhaustion is starting to creep back into my bones. "But right now, I need to rest."

Manny sighs and stands, squeezing my hand once more as a silent promise. Sara rises, nodding in agreement, and the two of them head toward the door.

"We'll be right here if you need anything. I'll come to bed in a bit," Sara says, glancing back at me.

When the door clicks shut, silence wraps around me once more. I lie back, staring at the ceiling. My mind spins with a million questions. Julian. His face, his touch—they felt so real. Too real.

I clutch the blankets tighter. He came when I needed him.

But how?

The question lingers briefly, but I'm too tired to give it much thought. Exhaustion pulls me under, and I drift into sleep—peaceful, with no dreams to haunt me tonight.

CHAPTER 22

Morning arrives with a soft glow filtering through the curtains, casting muted shades of gold across the room. I wake slowly, feeling Sara's presence beside me, her breathing slow and even.

The events of last night settle over me. The only thing keeping me from believing I've gone mad is the fact that Manny received a call from Julian. Julian was there. There's no doubt about it. It's both comforting and unnerving.

For a few moments, I stay in bed, listening to the quiet sounds of the house waking around me. But I know I can't linger here. I have to deal with the events from last night.

Carefully, I slip out of bed, not wanting to disturb Sara. She stirs slightly, mumbling something in her sleep, then settles back into the blankets, her face serene. I feel a pang of envy at how easily she sleeps.

I run a hand through my hair, as if trying to shake the thought loose, and quietly step out of the room.

Downstairs, the scent of fresh coffee greets me. Manny sits at the kitchen table, scrolling through his phone with a furrowed brow. At the sound of my footsteps he looks up, his expression softening with a mix of relief and concern.

"Morning, Elle. ¿Cómo te sientes?" he asks gently.

"Mejor," I say, offering a small smile as I pour myself a cup. "Just tired. Last night was… a lot.

I stare down at the chipped coffee mug in my hands, the one I haven't touched in months. It was Julian's favorite, a souvenir from our honeymoon in Thailand. The bitter scent of coffee fills my senses, pulling me back to memories of Julian laughing in this very kitchen, telling me some silly joke I can't quite remember. My fingers tighten around the handle.

"We can head to the doctor after we're done with breakfast," Manny says, pulling me from my thoughts. His voice is calm, but I can see the tension in his jaw, the protective worry he can't quite hide. "And I'll handle the report—we just need to make sure you're okay."

The thought of reliving the incident, of explaining everything, sends a shiver through me. But I know he's right.

"Ya sé," I murmur. "I'll make an appointment this morning."

Manny nods, looking relieved but still on edge. "Good. I don't want to take any chances."

A few minutes later, Sara joins us, hair tousled from sleep, her face brightening when she sees me. "Morning, Elle. How are you feeling?" She pulls out a chair and sits beside me.

"I'm okay," I reply, trying to sound reassuring. "I'm going to see the doctor today, just to be safe."

Sara reaches over and squeezes my hand, her eyes full of quiet relief. "Good. Todo va a salir bien."

The rest of the morning passes in a blur of phone calls and preparations. Manny handles reporting the incident, while Sara insists on coming with me to the doctor. I don't argue. I let them take charge, going along with their plans, though my mind is elsewhere—replaying Julian's words from last night, each revelation unraveling a new question.

The doctor's waiting room is small and quiet, the walls painted in soothing shades of blue. I sit beside Sara, fidgeting with the strap of my bag, trying to ignore the anxiety gnawing at me. When the nurse finally calls my name, I stand on shaky legs, feeling Sara's reassuring gaze as I follow the nurse into the examination room.

The doctor, a middle-aged woman with kind eyes and a gentle demeanor, enters a few moments later. She glances at her clipboard, then looks up, her gaze warm and steady. "So, Elle, I understand you had a bit of a scare last night."

"Yes," I reply, keeping my voice even. "I was drugged, but I'm not sure with what. I just want to make sure everything's okay."

She nods sympathetically. "Of course. We'll run some tests to check for any lingering effects, and I'll ask you a few questions about how you're feeling overall."

She proceeds with the examination, checking my vitals, asking me about symptoms, and ordering a blood test to identify the substance. I focus on her words, on the routine of it all, trying to push aside the questions about Julian that linger in my mind. For now, I need to be in the here and now.

"Physically, you seem to be fine," the doctor says, offering a gentle smile. "We'll have the test results in a day or two, but there's no immediate cause for concern. That said, it might help to talk to someone—a therapist, perhaps—about what happened. Experiences like this can leave lasting effects."

I nod, though I know the source of my anxiety goes far beyond what any therapist could address. "Thank you."

When I return to the waiting room, Sara is there, her face full of unspoken questions. I offer her a small smile, squeezing her hand. "Todo está bien," I say, keeping my tone as casual as possible.

On the way home, Sara chatters about the doctor's visit, about dinner plans, about anything but last night. I'm grateful for it—grateful for her comforting presence and her ability to fill the silence with something light, even if I'm not fully listening.

As strange as last night was, I have a feeling it's only going to get stranger.

CHAPTER 23

Dr. Rivera watches me closely, her pen resting lightly against her notebook, waiting for me to continue telling her about everything I've gone through since our last session.

"It sounds like you've been through a lot," she says gently, breaking the silence. "Have you heard back about your test results?"

I nod. "I did. They said it was a common date drug."

She nods thoughtfully, her expression calm but concerned. "And the man who tried to harm you—have the police been able to identify him?"

"No," I say, the word tasting bitter on my tongue. I pause, the memory of Manny breaking the news to me flashing through my mind.

The police couldn't find anything on the security cameras. Coincidentally, the cameras were down around the time everything happened. No footage. No leads. Nobody could identify the man, and no one remembered seeing him based on the description I gave. It's like he never existed.

Dr. Rivera leans forward slightly. "What about your brother, Manny? How is he processing the call he received from… Julian?"

She doesn't say it with doubt or skepticism, just careful consideration. She hasn't dismissed what I experienced or tried to rationalize it away. That alone makes it easier to answer her questions.

"He's … having a hard time trying to explain it," I say, thinking back to the way Manny struggled to make sense of what had happened.

It had taken him two days to bring it up. We were alone in the kitchen when he finally gathered the courage to ask me about it.

"I've tried to find an explanation for what happened the other night," he said, his voice low, his eyes searching mine. "But no matter how much I think about it … It was Julian. *Era él.*"

He'd stared at me like I held the answers, like I could somehow make sense of it all for him. But I couldn't. I couldn't explain it to him, just like I couldn't explain it to myself.

In the end, Manny had written it off as a miracle, a sign that Julian was watching over me. "How many stories have we heard about things like this growing up?" he'd said, more to himself than to me.

But none of those tales ever involved a loved one manifesting so vividly—so tangibly—that they could physically pull someone out of a bathroom.

"And what do *you* think?" she asks, her gaze soft but gentle.

"I … I don't know. Things from that night are still a little fuzzy," I say, lying.

I can't tell her the truth. If I did, she'd think I've really lost my mind. She'd suggest medication or some kind of treatment. But I'm not crazy. I know there's something happening. My gut is telling me to keep it to myself, to hold onto it quietly. If I voice my thoughts, if I say the words out loud, nobody will understand.

Dr. Rivera studies me for a moment, resting her pen on her notebook. "You've gone through so much lately," she says finally. "This incident, on top of everything else, adds to the weight you're already carrying. Why don't we end early today? Give yourself some space to process everything."

Relief sweeps over me, and I nod. "Yeah, that sounds good."

She offers me a small, warm smile. "Take care of yourself, Elle. We'll talk again next week."

I grab my purse and thank her before heading out to the lobby, my mind still swirling with everything I've chosen not to say.

Today, it's Manny who picks me up. Sara was called into work at the last minute, so he offered to come instead.

I spot him pacing back and forth on a narrow strip of grass in front of his car, phone pressed to his ear. His expression is tense, frustration etched across his face. It must be something to do with work.

As soon as he sees me, he mutters a quick goodbye, hangs up, and slips his phone into his pocket. "How was it?" he asks, walking over and opening the passenger door for me.

"Good," I reply, sliding into the seat.

Manny climbs into the driver's side and starts the car. The low hum of the engine fills the silence between us. For a few moments, neither of us says anything, but I can feel him glancing at me out of the corner of his eye, debating whether to say something.

Finally, as we pull out of the parking lot, he breaks the silence. "¿Seguro que estás bien?"

I force a small smile, turning to look out the window. "I'm fine, Manny. Really."

I know he doesn't believe me. Instead, after a beat, he clears his throat. "What if we have a movie night? We can grab dinner on the way home," he suggests, breaking the awkwardness.

I glance at him, surprised by the offer. "I love that idea. What about Sara?"

"She'll be getting off in about an hour. She found someone to cover the later shift."

"Nice," I say, the idea of something normal—something soothing—settling over me. "How long has it been since she started working at the labor and delivery unit?" I ask, remembering that Sara had been promoted a while back.

"Four months," Manny replies, his voice casual.

"Has it been that long?" I mutter, mostly to myself.

I fall quiet after that, the realization hitting me like a dull ache. *Four months.* This is the second time I've realized how much I don't know what's going on in my sibling's lives. It feels like there's this growing distance between us, one I don't know how to close.

"What do you want to eat?" Manny asks, pulling me out of my thoughts.

"Hmmm … How about Thai?"

"Thai it is. Mind placing the order? Text Sara and see what she wants, too."

I nod, pulling out my phone and doing as he asks.

After we pick up the food, we head home. The car fills with the smell of curry and basil from the bags in the back seat. As Manny turns onto our street, headlights flash in the rearview mirror.

"Looks like perfect timing," Manny says as Sara's car pulls into the driveway moments after us.

We step out of the car, and Sara climbs out of hers, looking tired but smiling when she sees us. She walks over and grabs one of the bags from Manny's hand.

The three of us make our way into the house together, the smell of food filling the air as we unpack everything in the kitchen. For a brief moment, it feels like old times—before everything changed, before grief and uncertainty carved this quiet distance between us.

We settle in the living room, plates balanced on our laps. Since we couldn't agree on a movie, Manny took it upon himself to pick one. A few minutes in, I realize it's one we've seen countless times—a story about the world falling apart in some unstoppable, catastrophic event. Normally, it's just mindless entertainment, a thrilling escape, but tonight it feels different. I can't explain it, but I have a strong feeling that this is like a warning. Almost like a sign.

I try to push the thought aside, forcing myself to relax. *It's just a movie. There's no hidden message behind it,* I tell myself.

Still, my mind wanders. If it is a sign, what could it mean? No, my feelings are just heightened from everything I've been through. Nothing more.

I glance at Manny, his face lit by the glow of the TV, his expression more at ease than it's been in days. Sara sits cross-legged on the couch, focused on her food but occasionally sneaking glances at the screen, her lips curling into a small smile at familiar parts of the movie.

For now, I let myself sink into the moment, into the small comfort of being here with them. Whatever the world is trying to tell me—or whatever I'm imagining—it can wait.

CHAPTER 24

Angry voices drag me from the dark abyss of unconsciousness. They feel familiar, pulling me toward a trio I can almost see. As I get closer, the urgency in their voices tightens my chest. Whatever they're discussing, it feels important. Something has happened.

"Do you realize what you've done?" The angelic woman's voice cuts through the air like a blade, her cerulean eyes blazing as she glares at Julian, who stands across from her and the beautiful man.

Julian's expression is tight with frustration. "If I hadn't stepped in, that man was going to assault her!" He takes a step forward, his voice rising. "Besides, I didn't know I was going to become solid… it just happened. I could feel her fear, her desperation, and before I knew it, I was there."

My heart skips a beat. Are they talking about the night of the incident? But that happened days ago. I take a step closer, staying in the shadows, unwilling to interrupt.

The beautiful man, standing between them, raises a hand to stop the argument before it escalates. "None of this should've been possible, but yelling at Julian won't help us now," he says, his voice calm. His hazel eyes flick between Julian and the woman, and I catch it—a flicker of concern, deep and unspoken, etched into his features. "We need to figure out what's happening. Fast."

Julian exhales sharply, his frustration simmering. He nods reluctantly. "Is this connected to… *them*?" he asks, his voice lower, a note of dread creeping in.

Them?

The beautiful man hesitates, shaking his head slowly. His posture is stiff, his uncertainty visible. "I don't know. But until they have her in their hands, she's going to find herself in dangerous situations. Again and again."

Her? My stomach twists. Are they talking about me? No, they can't be. Right? But deep down, I know the answer.

I want to step forward, to demand answers, but I stop myself. If I speak up, they'll send me away. They won't let me stay, and I'll never find out what's really going on.

The angelic woman's piercing eyes shift suddenly, locking onto mine. A chill races down my spine. *She sensed me, again.*

I freeze, my breath catching in my throat. Before I can move, the world around them shatters like glass, splintering into a thousand fragments.

I jolt awake, my heart pounding, my hands trembling. I'm back in my room.

My mind spins, trying to make sense of what I just saw. *Was it just a dream?* That's what I've been telling myself, isn't it? That they're just dreams. That there's no special meaning behind them. That I'm not special.

But then I glance at my phone. The screen lights up with the time, it's 5:55 a.m.

That number again. 555.

I stare at it, my pulse quickening. Is it still just a coincidence? Or am I looking for signs where there are none? Searching for answers I desperately want to believe exist?

Ugh. I rub my temples, trying to make the creeping ache into my head disappear.

"Elle?" Sara's voice startles me as she opens the bathroom door, flooding the room with soft light.

I blink a few times, adjusting to the brightness. "Morning," I mumble.

"What are you doing up so early?" she asks, stepping into the room and tying her hair back.

I hesitate. "Honestly? I don't know," I say. There's no way I'm telling her about the dream.

"You should try to sleep a little longer," she says. "It's barely morning."

"Yeah, maybe," I reply, though I know I won't.

She disappears back into the bathroom, and I lie back against the pillows, staring at the ceiling. The shards of the dream replay in my mind—the argument, Julian's words, the dread in their voices. *Them.*

Whatever it is, whatever they're hiding, I can feel it getting closer. Whatever *it* is.

And for the first time, I wonder if this is only the beginning.

CHAPTER 25

"It's been more than a week since the incident. How do you feel?" Dr. Rivera asks as our session begins.

Has it only been a week? It feels like ages ago. Nothing new has come up—no leads, no answers, and, strangely, no more dreams. Everything has gone eerily quiet.

"I feel … okay," I say, my fingers instinctively moving to my wedding ring. I twist it slowly, the familiar motion grounding me.

It's become a habit. Every time I come to therapy, as soon as the session starts, I find myself twisting the ring. Dr. Rivera never mentions it, never draws attention to it. She simply lets me do it.

"You've gone through a traumatic experience," she says. "And that's on top of everything else you've already been carrying. We've worked through the reasons that led you to want to take your own life, and we've found ways to help you manage your grief on the harder days. Last week, I asked you, what does grief mean to you? Have you thought about it?"

I hesitate, my fingers tightening around the ring. The question lingers in the space between us. Finally, I look up at her.

"Grief makes me feel alone," I admit quietly. "I've lost who I am. Sometimes I catch glimpses of myself in the mirror or in a reflection, and I don't recognize that person anymore. It's like I'm a stranger to myself."

Dr. Rivera nods, her pen moving across the page of her notebook. She doesn't interrupt, giving me space to say what I need to.

When she speaks, her voice is reassuring. "That's a powerful insight, Elle. And it's an important step—acknowledging how grief has affected your sense of self. It's not easy to confront that."

I continue, "It's not just about me, though. It's like I don't know how to be around other people anymore—around the people who still care about me." My voice wavers. "Emily keeps calling, keeps trying. She's my best friend, and I know she just wants to help. But every time I see her name on my screen, I can't bring myself to answer. Keeping my distance feels easier, but it's not fair to her."

Dr. Rivera holds my gaze, empathy in her expression. "That's an important realization, Elle. Recognizing how grief has shaped both your identity and your relationships is a significant step. Facing it isn't easy, but it's necessary."

I stay quiet, letting her words sink in.

She continues, "This week, I want you to focus on practicing self-care. I'd like you to start small—take walks, even if it's just around the block. Begin journaling. Write about your thoughts, your feelings, anything that comes to mind. We've worked hard to manage your grief, and I think you've reached a place where we can begin focusing on *you*. It's time to start finding who you are now, because you won't be the person you were before the grief. And that's okay. Learning to accept that will take time, but it's a journey we can work through together."

Her words stir something in me—hope, maybe, or at least the faint possibility of it.

Dr. Rivera leans forward slightly, her expression kind but serious. "I want to leave you with something to think about. How can you show yourself kindness and compassion today? Ask yourself that question every day moving forward. Can you do that?"

I hesitate for a moment, then nod. "Yeah, I can do that."

She offers me a small smile. "Good. One step at a time, Elle. You're doing the work, and that's what matters."

As I leave the session, her question stays with me, circling in my mind. How can I show myself kindness and compassion today?

It's a really good question—one I don't have an answer to. I've been neglecting myself ever since Julian passed away. Somewhere along the way, I forgot what it means to care for myself. To show myself even a shred of kindness.

Where would I even start? How would that look like? But I guess that's where Dr. Rivera comes in, to help guide me.

And maybe, just maybe, I'll figure out how to show myself some compassion.

CHAPTER 26

It takes me two days to finally bring myself to take a walk.

On the first day, I almost did. I had my shoes on, the laces tied tightly, ready to step out the door. But then I froze. The thought of walking through the neighborhood, passing neighbors that know me. Who might glance at me, nod at me, or—worst of all—ask me how I'm doing … It was too much. I kicked off my shoes and told myself I'd try again tomorrow.

Tomorrow came and went.

But today, as the sunlight filters through the windows and the quiet hum of the house settles around me, I finally push myself out the door. I don't think. I just go.

The warm air brushes against my skin as I step onto the sidewalk. It's mid-morning, and the neighborhood is calm, almost serene. A few cars pass by, the soft rumble of their engines fading into the background. Birds chirp in the distance, and for a moment, I focus on the sound, letting it drown out the noise in my head.

My feet move slowly at first, like I'm testing the ground beneath me. The familiarity of it all—the houses, the trees, the neatly trimmed lawns—feels strange, almost like I'm walking through a memory of a place I used to know.

I decide to walk at least a block and see how I feel after that.

At the corner of the block, I pause, taking in a deep breath and letting it out slowly. My hands fidget, reaching instinctively for my wedding ring. I twist it absentmindedly as I glance up at the sky. The clouds are soft and wispy, shifting lazily across a blue sky.

A rare sense of peace washes over me—something I haven't felt in a long time.

Dr. Rivera really knows what she's talking about. I had my doubts at first, but she has really come through.

I've learned to manage my grief, to be in the present, and now, to do things I didn't think I could anymore—especially alone. I guess this is what my life is going to look like now. Doing things on my own.

By the time I get back to the house, I feel lighter. My legs ache, but it's a good ache. The kind that reminds you you've done something for yourself.

As I approach the door, Sara pulls into the driveway. She looks exhausted, her hair pulled back in a loose bun, her scrubs slightly wrinkled. Graveyard shift. It's been a while since she worked nights, which meant I'd had the room to myself for once.

"Buenos días," she calls, stifling a yawn as she steps out of the car.

"Buenos días," I reply, holding the door open for her.

She pauses, giving me a curious look. "You went out?"

"Just for a walk," I say, a small smile tugging at my lips.

Sara raises an eyebrow, her expression softening. "Qué bien por ti. Me alegra que empieces a hacer algo por ti misma."

I nod, offering her another small smile, one that feels just a little more real than before.

"¿Te vas a dormir luego o te vas a bañar?" I ask as Sara sets her travel mug in the dishwasher.

"A dormir," she replies, letting out a dramatic sigh. "It's been a long night."

"¡Cochina! You're going to stink up the bed!" I call after her, a teasing grin spreading across my face as she heads for the stairs.

She laughs, shaking her head as she disappears up to our room.

I walk to the kitchen to make myself another cup of coffee and settle onto the couch, the warmth of the mug seeping into my hands.

I turn on the TV, letting the soft murmur of a show fill the quiet space, more for background noise than anything else. The smell of freshly brewed coffee floats in the air. It makes me feel relaxed.

I take a few slow sips of my coffee. My eyelids grow heavier with each sip. Before I know it, my head tilts back against the cushion, and the world around me blurs as sleep takes over.

I'm running. My breath comes in heavy bursts, my heart pounding with panic. But I'm not myself—I'm a brown bear, and I have a cub.

Something is chasing us. The dark figures behind us are growing closer, shadowy masses shifting as they move. We're trapped. Panic courses through my body, sharp and unrelenting. I know, deep in my bones, that I must protect my cub at all costs.

The figures—no, the *beasts*—have cornered us. They herd us toward a frozen river, their forms blurring into shapes I can't quite make out. Now I see the snow surrounding us, blanketing the ground.

I nuzzle my cub, communicating reassurance. *Everything is going to be okay.* I don't know if I believe it, but I have to keep my cub calm. The beasts don't attack. Instead, they gather in a loose circle several feet away, their backs against us. It's as if they know we won't go anywhere.

Suddenly, a herd of elk appears, their massive antlers glinting in the pale light. But they're not like any elk I've ever seen. Their antlers are dark, thick, and twisted, almost like ancient tree branches. They step forward, and I understand they're here to help.

There are no words between us, but we understand each other perfectly. They offer to help us cross the frozen river to the other side, where safety waits. Desperation claws at me, and I nod—if that's even something a bear can do.

The elk pull me and my cub across the ice with a rope looped around their antlers. Their hooves clatter against the frozen surface, every step echoing into the still air. Anxiety claws at the edges of my mind. *What if the beasts notice we're escaping?*

The ice groans beneath us. Cracks spiderweb across the surface, the jagged lines growing with every step. My breath fogs the air as I try to warn the elk. I try to tell them to hurry because the ice is breaking. But all I can manage is to huff, and the elk don't pay attention to me. They keep walking across unhurried and calm, almost as if this is their way of letting me know that it's going to be okay.

I can see the other side of the bank; we're so close. But that's when the ice gives way with a deafening crack. My cub yelps as it slips from my grasp, tumbling into the freezing water below.

Panic surges through me. Without hesitation, I dive in. The water hits me like a thousand needles, stealing the breath from my lungs as the current claws at me, trying to pull my cub away. But I won't let it. I *can't* let it go. My paws stretch out, and I grab hold, clutching the small, shivering body against me as I kick furiously toward the surface.

Breaking through the water, gasping for air, I swim with every ounce of strength I have. My claws scrape the edge of the riverbank, and with a final, desperate heave,

I pull us both onto solid ground. My cub is shaking but alive. Relief floods through me.

Then I hear it—the beasts. They've noticed. Their roars cut through the air as they charge toward us.

I push my cub forward, signaling it to go. It scrambles up the snowy incline where the elk are waiting. But when I glance back at them, they're no longer elk. Their antlers no longer twist and stretch. They have somehow detached from the former elk and have transformed into tall, slim tree trunks that rise from the ground. What used to be elk have been replaced by human beings. They stand silently in white linen robes, their expressions unreadable.

I spin around to face the charging beasts—but they, too, have changed. They're no longer beasts but humans, cloaked in black robes. Their faces are barely visible under the hood that covers their head.

And then I notice something else, the fear that had consumed me moments ago is gone. I straighten, realizing the truth. *I'm not afraid anymore.*

I glance down at myself. My paws are gone, replaced by hands. My fingers tremble as I flex them, feeling the familiar strength of my human form once again.

Turning back to the figures below, I plant my feet firmly on the ground. My voice rings out, fierce and defiant, "We're not afraid of you!"

I walk over to one of the tree trunks—the smooth, cylindrical remnants of the elk—and kick it loose. It snaps easily under my foot, tumbling down the hill with a hollow crack. The trunk crashes into the leader, striking it square in the chest and knocking it to the ground.

The others stop, frozen. They look at their fallen leader, I can see how they hesitate as they look at one another trying to figure out what to do now that they've seen that their leader is not invincible.

"You don't have to follow him!" I shout to them, my voice cutting through the still air. "You can decide for yourselves!"

For a moment, silence takes over. Within moments, the snow melts away, and a meadow begins to take its place. What felt like a wintry day just seconds ago now feels like the height of summer—warm, golden, and alive.

I turn toward my cub, but it's no longer a cub. It's a baby, nestled in a soft bed of grass. My heart swells as I reach down and pick it up, cradling it in my arms.

"In due time, you will have to make the choice, and it will decide the future of your child," a voice says.

I turn toward the speaker—the man who had been the elk that helped us across the river. A bright glow radiates behind him, so blinding that I can't make out his features. But somehow, I understand him perfectly.

I don't speak. Instead, I nod, holding my baby closer.

I open my eyes slowly, my mind hazy with sleep. It takes a few seconds to register my surroundings—the couch beneath me, the faint murmur of the TV, the now-cold cup of coffee sitting on the table.

Of all the dreams I've had, this one is by far the strangest.

I try to hold on to the details, but they're already slipping away, dissolving like mist in the morning sun. The only thing that stays with me, carved into my mind, is what the man said, *You will have to make a choice, and it will decide the future of your child.*

Which is odd since I don't have a child. I doubt I'll have one anytime soon. Not with Julian gone. *Dead husband and all.*

A laugh escapes me suddenly. I know it's not the time to laugh, but the idea of me having a child now, after losing my true love, is absurd. Funny even, in a cruel, twisted way.

I shake my head, the smile fading as quickly as it came. I'm still processing my grief, still learning how to exist in a world without him. Dreams are just dreams. Nothing more.

At least that's what I keep telling myself.

But as I sit there, staring at the cold coffee and listening to the hum of the TV, a quiet voice at the back of my mind whispers something I can't ignore.

What if it's not?

CHAPTER 27

The rest of the week goes by without any strange dreams or whispers. I've started to fall into a routine—morning walks for at least 20–30 minutes, followed by journaling when I get back. Tuesdays and Thursdays are reserved for my therapy sessions at 5:00 p.m.

Everything feels normal. But since last night, I've started getting a nagging feeling that this isn't going to last, and I'm afraid.

I shake the feeling off as I walk into the house after my morning walk. The scent of fresh brewed coffee greets me, and I find Sara in the kitchen, moving around as she preps breakfast.

"Where's Manny?" I ask, settling at the table to watch her. She's always been quick in the kitchen, her movements fluid and confident.

"He had to go to the office really quick," she replies, not looking up as she chops an onion.

"On a Saturday?" I ask, confused.

"There's some huge project, y tenía que entregarle algo a alguien. No sé exactamente," she says with a small shrug, her focus still on the cutting board.

For a moment, I sit in silence, watching her work. There's something I've been meaning to bring up, but I haven't found the right time. Or maybe I've just been avoiding it.

"Sara …" I start, hesitating. "I've been thinking. Since I've been working on myself lately and taking steps forward to move on with my life … maybe it's time I started sleeping on my own again."

Sara freezes mid-chop, the knife hovering above the onion. She looks up at me slowly, her brows knitting together as she processes my words. "A ver, espérame. ¿Qué es lo que quieres?"

I take a deep breath, my fingers fidgeting with the edge of the table. "I think it's time for me to get my room back to myself."

For a moment, she just stares at me, her expression unreadable. Then, a smile begins to spread across her face. She sets the knife down and walks over to me. Taking a seat next to me, she pulls me into a hug.

"¡Claro que sí!" she says, her voice warm and full of pride. "I know how much work you've been putting in. I think you deserve to have some space to yourself." She pulls back slightly, taking my hands in hers. "I know Manny and I have been hard on you. Maybe too hard. And it might have felt suffocating at times. But it's only because we love you. We've already lost so much, and we didn't want to lose you too."

Her words hit me like a punch to the chest. My heart sinks, guilt unfurling in the pit of my stomach.

I don't know what to say.

"Sara …" I manage, but my voice falters.

She shakes her head, her hands squeezing mine. "No, no. Don't feel bad. You've come so far, Elle. Let's not dwell on the past. It happened, and the only thing we can do is move forward."

I swallow hard and nod, unable to say more.

Sara releases me and stands. "You can help me move my stuff back," she says over her shoulder. "Maybe we can make it a little cozier for me—I've been wanting to redecorate anyway."

I let out a small laugh, though the knot in my stomach doesn't fully loosen.

After breakfast, Sara and I begin moving her things out of my room and back into the one down the hall, across from Manny's. It doesn't take long—most of her stuff is already there anyway.

By the time we're done, it's already dinner time. We had skipped lunch, too caught up in rearranging the furniture and unpacking to notice the hours slipping by.

The sound of the front door closing echoes from downstairs.

"Sara? Elle?" Manny's voice calls out.

"Up here!" we both yell back in unison, exchanging a quick grin.

A few moments later, Manny appears in the doorway, his arms crossed and a confused look on his face.

"¿Y esto, qué?" he asks, raising an eyebrow.

"I'm moving out. ¿No ves?" Sara replies sarcastically.

Manny shoots her a scolding look. "Sí veo eso. But why all of a sudden"

"It's time, don't you think?" Sara says as she glances at me. "Elle has been doing great! I think it's only fair she gets her space back."

She's doing all the talking so I don't have to, and for that, I'm grateful. I watch as my siblings bicker back and forth. Making me feel warm inside.

I smile as their bickering continues. It's always been like this since we were kids—Sara pushing Manny's buttons, Manny pretending to be exasperated. Some things, it seems, never change. And I'm happy about that.

"So, since you two have been busy with all this," Manny says, gesturing at the room with a raised eyebrow, "I'm assuming there's no dinner?"

"And you would be correct," Sara responds without missing a beat, shooting him a smug look.

"What do you think if we go out to eat?" he offers.

"¿Tú vas a pagar?" Sara asks, her voice suddenly giddy, her playful grin widening.

"Yes, yes," Manny replies, already turning to head back downstairs.

Sara claps her hands together like she's won a prize, then winks at me. "Let's go before he changes his mind."

I smile as I follow Sara out of her room. It's been a long time since something as simple as dinner felt this easy.

CHAPTER 28

"Isabella," a raspy voice calls out in the distance.

I'm on the cold, hard ground, rocking back and forth, my arms wrapped tightly around my knees. Tears stream down my face and sobs rack my chest. A few feet away, I see Manny and Sara sprawled on the ground, their limbs twisted at strange angles, like they've been dropped from the sky. Their bodies lifeless.

"This is your doing, Isabella," the voice hisses, closer now.

"No," I whimper. Tears blur my vision as I rock harder, my mind clinging to the rhythm as if it could shield me from the truth. "No."

The ground beneath me trembles, low and ominous, and I freeze. The cold earth feels unstable, shifting beneath me. Heat begins to rise, seeping through the widening cracks as the sharp, choking scent of burning sulfur fills the air.

Then, the ground splits open.

My breath catches as I watch in horror. The lifeless bodies of my siblings slide toward the fissures, disappearing into the fiery depths below.

"No!" I scream, scrambling forward, but it's too late. The earth swallows them whole.

Fissures spread further, jagged and glowing with an angry, molten light, as if the very ground is alive—writhing, furious, and hungry.

From one of the largest cracks, something emerges.

At first, it's just a faint shimmer—dark and oily, like smoke that clings to the air. But then it grows. A hand claws its way out, skeletal and charred, the fingers curling into the dirt as it pulls itself upward. Another hand follows.

I choke on a scream as the first figure rises, its hollow eyes locking onto mine. They burn with fiery hunger, glowing like embers beneath a blackened skull.

And it's not alone.

Dozens of hands follow, clawing, grasping, dragging themselves out of the fiery pit. One by one, the creatures emerge. Their bodies are blackened, their shapes shifting unnaturally, as if they can't decide what they are. Some have limbs that stretch impossibly long, others have mouths that yawn open too wide, filled with jagged, mismatched teeth. All of them crawl toward me.

Panic surges through me like lightning. I scramble backward, my hands scraping against the jagged ground. My breath comes in shallow, gasping bursts.

Then, I hear it.

A new sound pierces the air—a chorus of gut-wrenching screams. My head snaps up, and I see glowing orbs of light, bursting into existence all around me. They zoom past me, fast and frantic, like shooting stars in reverse.

The orbs descend into the pit, colliding with the fire. For every creature that crawled out, a ball of light replaces it. The light sinks into the flames, disappearing into the inferno.

I realize with a jolt that the lights are *souls*.

Their screams echo in my ears, filled with anguish and despair, as they are drawn into the pit, consumed by the fire. The creatures climbing out pay no attention. They move forward, unrelenting, their glowing eyes fixed on me.

I can't stop it. I can't stop *any of it*.

"No …" I whisper, my voice breaking as terror grips me. My hands dig into the ground as I push myself further back. "No!"

The creatures crawl closer, their movements jerky and unnatural, inching toward me with each second. My breath comes in shallow gasps, and I brace myself for the inevitable. But then, they stop—just a foot away from me.

They freeze, their glowing eyes fixed on me, their twisted bodies motionless as if they're waiting. Waiting for me to tell them what to do.

The voice returns, harsh and mocking, filling my head like a taunting echo.

"You can't run from this, Isabella. You can't undo what's been done. This is your doing. This is your fate."

"No, it's not!" I yell, shaking my head furiously.

Suddenly, a dark figure materializes beside me, cloaked in flowing black robes. Its face is concealed beneath the deep shadow of a hood. The air turns ice-cold, suffocating, and I stifle a scream as my body tenses with dread.

"This is your fate, Isabella," the figure says, its voice low and reverberating, like it's coming from the depths of the earth. "Together, we'll bring forth our new world."

The words send a chill down my spine. I scramble backwards, desperate to escape, but the ground beneath me crumbles without warning, breaking apart into fiery shards.

I scream as the earth gives way entirely, and I tumble into the abyss.

The air rushes past me, hot and oppressive, as flames lick at the rim of the gorge. Above me, the figure's hooded silhouette looms at the edge of the crumbling ground. A menacing laugh echoes through the void, chilling.

"The time is coming, Isabella," the voice calls after me, growing fainter but no less terrifying. "You can't run away from it."

The fire closes in around me, and I thrash, desperate to stop my descent, my hands clawing at nothing but empty air.

I wake up gasping, my hands flailing in the darkness, desperate to grab hold of something solid.

My chest heaves as I sit up, running trembling hands through my damp hair. My heart pounds violently in my chest, and I force myself to take deep breaths. *It was just a dream. It was just a dream,* I repeat silently, over and over.

Was it?

Yes! I snap at myself. *Yes, it was just a dream!*

My thoughts churn, the nightmare still vivid behind my eyes. The sensation of falling refuses to fade, leaving me unsettled, as if the ground beneath me could give way at any moment. The dream feels like a warning of something that's coming.

It's just a dream!

I can feel the edges of an anxiety attack crawling up my spine, its icy grip spreading through my chest. My breathing becomes shallow, and my thoughts spiral faster, out of control.

Julian.

His name is the first thing that bursts through the chaos, clear and sharp like a beacon in the dark.

"Chave?"

That voice—*his* voice. And then I see him.

There, in the shadows of my room, standing to the left of my bed. His form is unmistakable, barely illuminated by the pale light sneaking through the curtains.

My breath hitches. My heart skips.

I blink—once, twice—but he doesn't disappear. He's still there. My Julian.

For a moment, I'm frozen. I want to scream—not out of fear, but out of sheer disbelief. But I stop myself. If I scream, Manny and Sara will come rushing in, and I have no idea how to explain this.

"Julian …" I whisper, my voice trembling.

He steps forward, his form barely illuminated. "I don't know how this is happening," he murmurs, as if trying to make sense of it himself. "But I'm here, Chave. I'm here."

All I can do is stare, my mind struggling to reconcile what I'm seeing with what I know should be impossible. Julian, standing in front of me. Real. Solid. Alive … in some way.

I don't know whether to cry or reach out for him— or both.

CHAPTER 29

I scramble across the bed toward Julian, my heart pounding with desperate urgency. Every movement feels like a race against time, as if he might vanish at any moment.

He meets me at the edge of the bed, and I reach out, my hand trembling, afraid he'll dissolve like smoke the moment I touch him. But he doesn't. Instead, Julian closes the distance, pulling me into his arms, his familiar warmth wrapping around me.

My breath catches, and before I know it, tears are streaming down my face. I bury myself in his shoulder, clutching at him.

"Julian," I whisper into his shirt, my voice cracking.

His embrace tightens, his hand tracing slow, soothing circles over my back. For a moment, everything else fades—the nightmare, the fear, even my racing thoughts. All that matters is that he's here, solid and warm and *real*.

When he gently pulls back, I resist, clinging to him like a lifeline. But Julian seems to sense my fear. He cups my face with his hands, his thumb brushing away the tears on my cheeks. His touch is warm and solid.

This isn't a dream, right?

"No, it's not a dream," Julian replies, as if reading my thoughts. "I don't know how it's possible, but I'm really here."

Relief floods my body, but my mind spins with questions. Julian guides me back to the bed, lying down beside me. I curl into him, burying my face in his chest. His familiar scent filling my nostrils. I feel whole, something I haven't felt in so long.

"Don't leave me again," I mumble into his shirt, my voice barely audible.

Julian strokes my hair gently, not saying a word, but the silence hangs between us. A reminder that whatever force brought him here could take him away just as quickly.

After a long pause, his voice breaks the quiet. "Chave," he murmurs, his tone pained, as if what he's about to say hurts him as much as it will hurt me. "There are things happening that go beyond what you can see … beyond the human world. I'm a part of those things. I shouldn't be here with you like this."

I pull back slightly, searching his face, my stomach twisting with a mixture of confusion and dread. "What are you saying?"

Julian hesitates, his expression shadowed, his eyes unreadable. "I'm your spiritual guide, Chave. I'm meant to protect you, to watch over you, but from a distance.

Whatever's allowing me to materialize like this—it's breaking rules. Rules that are important, even if I don't fully understand them."

He pauses, as if weighing how much more to reveal. "Your guardian angels … They're beside themselves trying to figure out what's happening. They're not happy with my involvement. They say it's causing an imbalance. But things are already unstable."

"An imbalance?" I echo. "What does that even mean?"

"There's a power struggle going on—something beyond what most people know or could ever understand. It's disrupting everything, blurring lines that shouldn't be crossed. And somehow …" He trails off, as if reluctant to say it out loud.

"Somehow, what?" I press.

He looks at me, his expression melts, his eyes filled with a sadness that makes my chest tighten. "It all centers around you."

"Me?" My heart sinks, my pulse racing with disbelief. "Julian, that doesn't make sense. Why would it center around me?"

"I don't know," he admits. "But everything that's happening—everything I've seen—it's because of you."

My mind spins, trying to piece together the fragments of the impossible truth he's laying before me. Guardian angels? Imbalance? Power struggles? None of it feels real, yet Julian's presence, his warmth, is undeniable. I swallow, the beginnings of a question forming on my lips.

"The dreams," I say, my voice barely a whisper, "the ones with you and those other beings … Those weren't dreams, were they?"

Julian's face darkens. "No," he admits quietly. "Somehow, you've been slipping into our realm. That shouldn't be possible, Chave. Not for someone like you. Someone *human*."

His words send a chill through me, but before I can ask what he means, another thought strikes.

"What about the other dreams? The ones with La Muerte?"

The change in Julian is immediate. His expression hardens, his jaw tightening as he sits up abruptly, pulling me with him. His hands grip my shoulders, his intensity pinning me in place.

"La Muerte?" he repeats, his voice low and tense. "What dreams, Chave? Tell me everything."

I start recounting all my dreams, beginning with the one where I tried to save him but failed. Julian listens intently, nodding occasionally, his expression serious and focused. He asks clarifying questions—specific details, what I felt, what I saw—and I do my best to answer each one.

When I finally finish, Julian exhales, leaning back slightly. His brows furrow, his expression troubled.

"I'm still new to all of this," he admits. "But your dreams have meaning, Chave. They're trying to tell you something." He pauses. "But I don't think I'm the one to give you answers. You need to talk to your guardian angels."

"Me? Talk to them?" I repeat, panic starts to bubble up. "How am I supposed to do that?!"

Julian reaches for my hands, squeezing them gently, his way of telling me everything will work out.

But will it? He's just dropped all this information on me, and I'm still trying to wrap my mind around it. Now he expects me to just *casually* connect with my guardian angels? How am I supposed to do that?

"Chave, you can do this. You need to trust yourself more. Your subconscious already knows how to guide you. You just have to let it." He says, giving me one of his crooked smiles I've missed so much.

It really *is* Julian. The way he looks at me, the way he speaks—it's him. Tears threaten to spill, but I blink them back, not wanting to fall apart.

A sudden knock at the door snaps me out of my thoughts, and my head whips toward it.

Before I can say anything, the door creaks open, and Sara pops her head in.

"I thought I heard you talking," she says, her brow furrowed with confusion. "Were you talking to someone?"

I glance back at Julian, but the space beside me is empty. The bed is cool, as if he was never there at all. My heart sinks, confusion swirling like a storm in my mind.

"Uh … I just woke up from a nightmare," I say, clambering for an explanation. "Maybe I was talking in my sleep."

Sara opens the door wider and steps into the room, her skeptical gaze flicking around. "What are you doing up, anyway?"

"What do you mean? It's …" I trail off, unsure of the time.

"It's 5:55 a.m.," she says. "I need to get to work."

555.

That number again. My stomach tightens. This can't be a coincidence.

"Oh," is all I manage to say, the word weak and hollow.

Sara gives me a quick glance. "Since you're good, I'll see you later. I'm running late. Text me if you need anything, okay?"

Without waiting for a response, she leaves, closing the door behind her.

I sit there for a moment, staring at the closed door. Then, slowly, I let myself fall back onto the bed, my body sinking into the mattress. My mind is a tangled mess, and nothing makes sense.

How was Julian here? How could he be here and then just … be gone?

I press my palms to my eyes, trying to make sense of it all. Did I make it up? Was I dreaming?

I don't know what's real anymore.

CHAPTER 30

The next couple of days, I go about my routine as usual. But when I'm alone in my room, I try to summon Julian—if that's even the right way to describe it. I call his name, but nothing happens.

I haven't been able to sleep much either, and when I do, the sleep is restless, dreamless. Julian told me to trust my subconscious, but my subconscious isn't leading me anywhere.

Tonight is no different. The house is quiet, except for the faint creaks of the floor settling. But sleep doesn't come. I lie there in the darkness, staring up at the ceiling, tracing the pale streaks of moonlight spilling through the curtains.

With a frustrated sigh, I roll over, tucking my arm beneath my pillow. The sheets feel cool against my skin, but they do little to soothe the storm in my mind.

Why can't I dream? Was it even real? Was he real?

I squeeze my eyes shut, forcing myself to start counting in a desperate attempt to calm my restless thoughts. One.

Two. Three. The numbers flow like a steady rhythm, pulling me deeper and deeper.

It works.

The familiar darkness wraps around me, solid and impenetrable, the same way it always does when I dream of my guardian angels and Julian. But this time, something feels different. The blackness isn't as complete as before.

Far in the distance, faint glimmers blink into existence, like tiny stars fighting to break through the void. They flicker teasing me with the promise of something beyond the darkness. Something just out of reach, but close.

I take a hesitant step forward.

The ground shifts beneath me, not solid but not entirely unstable either, as if it's breathing, responding to my movement. The air around me pulses gently like the realm itself is alive—watching, waiting.

My heartbeat thrums louder, filling the silence. I strain to hear anything else—anything familiar. But there's nothing. Just the thick, empty dark and the sound of my own ragged breathing.

"Hello?" I call out, my voice small and uncertain.

The darkness swallows my words, but they don't vanish entirely. Faint echoes bounce back to me, distorted and faint, as if the realm is deciding whether or not to answer.

Then, from somewhere deep in the blackness, I hear it—a soft, familiar voice, like a whisper carried on the wind.

But it's not Julian.

It's something else, it's a voice that's calling to something deep inside me. It stirs feelings that have been waiting in the core of my soul.

"Isabella," it murmurs, as soft as a memory. "You're close now. Just a little further."

I swallow, my throat suddenly dry. "Julian? Is that you?"

The silence that follows is heavy—but not empty. The voice doesn't answer, yet I *feel* it all around me, wrapping itself around my senses. It isn't harsh or cold—it's guiding, gentle. A quiet presence urges me forward, drawing me deeper into the darkness.

The faint lights ahead intensify with each step, revealing a path that wasn't there before. The lights pulse and flicker, casting shifting shadows that gradually take form—outlines emerging from the void.

Something vast and ancient lies ahead, hidden within the shadows.

I keep walking, driven by a force I can't explain. There's no fear now, only an unshakable pull, like a string tethered to my chest is drawing me closer to something I need to see, something waiting for me beyond the veil of darkness.

With each step, the landscape changes. The darkness pulling back like retreating tides, revealing more of what lies beneath.

The ground beneath my feet grows firmer, more stable, no longer shifting with every move I make. The suffocating blackness lifting little by little, unveiling more of the world around me.

The scattered lights start to merge, taking on shapes that grow sharper. I see the faint outlines of trees, their branches swaying in a breeze I can't feel. Distant mountains rise on the horizon, their jagged peaks cutting into a sky suspended between night and day—a twilight that seems endless.

The landscape unfolds before me like a half-remembered dream—surreal, fragmented, slipping just beyond my grasp. It's unlike anything I've ever seen, and yet it feels familiar, as though I've been here before.

In another life. Another time.

The feeling only deepens as I move forward, the lights guiding my steps. Though the voice has fallen silent, its presence lingers at the edge of my mind, an unspoken urge pushing me onward.

Then, I step into a clearing, and the darkness vanishes.

A soft, golden light spills over everything, warm and radiant, washing away the last traces of shadows. The air here feels alive, thrumming with a quiet energy—soothing and electric all at once. I inhale deeply, and all the tension in my body begins to unwind.

And then, I see her.

She stands at the center of the clearing, luminous and still.

It's her—the woman from my dreams. But now, she is more than a fleeting image. She is real, vivid, standing before me as if for the first time.

Her features are sharper now, her beauty otherworldly and breathtaking. She radiates a calm authority, a presence both commanding and gentle, as it flows effortlessly from her. She doesn't just stand in this place, she belongs to it. She feels woven from its light, as though the clearing itself exists because of her.

"You're her!" I exclaim, the words escaping before I can stop them, awe slipping into my voice. Every time she's appeared in my dreams, she's sent me back. Every time, without fail.

"Are you going to send me back like before?" I ask, bracing myself for the familiar sensation of being yanked back to my realm.

"No," she says, her voice laced with authority. It's a tone that leaves no room for doubt, no space for questions. "This time is different. There is much we must discuss."

She turns, her movement impossibly fluid, more like gliding than walking. The air around her shimmers in response, rippling as if it's alive, responsive to her presence.

"Follow me."

For a moment, I hesitate. But the pull to go with her is overwhelming—terrifying and irresistible all at once. It feels like being drawn toward a flame, knowing it might burn but unable to resist the light.

I take a cautious step forward, my feet barely making a sound against the firm ground. Then another.

Before I know it, I'm following her deeper into this strange, shifting landscape.

As we move deeper into the realm, I can't help but take in the strange, breathtaking beauty that surrounds us. The landscape feels boundless, dotted with fields of impossibly green grass that seem to sparkle under the strange light. Towering trees rise around us, their leaves shimmering in an otherworldly spectrum of silver and gold, catching and reflecting the glow of the sky.

It's unlike anything I've ever seen, and yet there's something achingly familiar about it, like a memory I can almost touch but can't quite grasp.

We walk in silence for a while, the only sounds are the soft rustling of leaves overhead and the gentle whisper of the wind as it weaves through the trees. I feel at peace here, something I haven't felt in months.

Then, a voice breaks the stillness.

"Chave, you made it!"

The sudden voice jolts me from my thoughts. I stop and turn, my heart skipping as I see him. Julian stands a few paces ahead, his familiar crooked smile lighting up his face. There's pride in his eyes, a warm, unguarded joy that lifts the last of my hesitation.

"Julian!" I exclaim, a smile of my own breaking free as I quicken my pace, unable to stop myself. I close the distance between us, and the moment his hand finds mine, everything else falls away.

"Que te dije?" he murmurs, his tone both teasing and proud.

"Tenías razón," I reply, rolling my eyes, though I can't suppress the smile tugging at my lips.

I glance back at the woman, who remains silent, those cerulean eyes fixed on me with a mixture of curiosity and expectation. "Where's the other guy?" I ask.

"Here," a deep, melodic voice answers from behind me.

I turn, and there he is—the beautiful man with strikingly symmetrical features and warm hazel eyes. His presence is magnetic, commanding in a way that makes me feel both drawn in and unnervingly small. Still, there's a tenderness about him, something that makes me feel safe.

He steps forward with smooth confidence, his eyes locking onto mine as though he can see straight through to my soul.

"Welcome, Isabella," he says, his voice echoing through the stillness.

I take a deep breath, bracing myself for what's next.

CHAPTER 31

I look between the three of them, unsure where to start or what to ask. My mind is swimming with too many questions, all crashing into one another.

"What do I even call you guys?" I blurt out, the words escaping before I can stop them. "Besides, you know, beautiful woman and man."

The man's lips twitch, like he's fighting back a laugh. Meanwhile, the woman remains composed, her expression calm and serious, her radiating authority making me feel self-conscious.

"You can call us A and E," the woman says, her tone smooth. "I'm A, and he's E."

I blink. "A and E?" I repeat, skeptical. "What kind of names are those?"

As soon as the words leave my mouth, I regret them. My hands fly up to cover my lips. *What the hell am I doing? Questioning angelic beings?*

The man—E—lets out a low chuckle. "Names imply control, and you don't have that over us. Our real names carry power, and they're not something you could even pronounce." He pauses, letting that sink in.

"And these forms," E continues, gesturing to himself and A, "aren't what we truly look like. We appear this way to make it easier for you. Trust me, if you saw us in our real forms …" He trails off, his expression playful yet cryptic.

I blink again, trying to process that. Not their true forms? *What does that even mean?*

¿Qué chingados? What the hell?

A cuts in, her voice steady. "It would be overwhelming. Perhaps even unbearable."

I glance between them, trying to wrap my mind around their words. These faces, these forms—they're for *me*. To make them less terrifying. I'm not sure it's working.

"I'm sure you have a lot of questions," A says, breaking the silence. "But what you really want to know is why this is happening to you."

She's right. That's the only question I care about. I nod, bracing myself for an answer I'm certain I won't like.

"There's more to the supernatural than humans understand," A begins, her tone unyielding. "Every realm—whether you call them worlds, dimensions, or something else—operates under a strict cosmic order. It is our duty to maintain that balance."

She pauses before continuing. "If that balance is disrupted, it can have catastrophic consequences. Every action, every choice, sends ripples through the fabric of existence. What happens in one realm affects all others, whether humanity realizes it or not."

I blink, struggling to process what she's saying. "Balance between what, exactly?"

"Between creation and destruction. Between light and darkness, life and death. The First, Second, and Third Comings all play a role in maintaining that balance." A's voice remains firm, unwavering.

"Think of the Second Coming as the in-between," E interjects. "It's the time between the First Coming and the Third Coming. A time for humanity to reflect, to prepare, to turn away from sin, and to choose redemption."

"Exactly," A says. "Humans have been given free will, and with it, the power to decide the course of their souls. The choices they make—how they fight their inner battles, whether they give in to temptation or rise above it—are shaping the world's readiness for what's to come."

"And the Third Coming?" I ask.

"The Third Coming is inevitable," A replies, her tone heavy with reverence. "It is the return of God's ultimate presence to the world. It will mark the fulfillment of the cosmic order—the final judgment, the restoration of all things." She pauses. "But humanity's choices will determine whether the Third Coming is met with salvation or destruction. And as you know, there is no precise timeline— time does not exist for God."

E steps closer, his hazel eyes meeting mine. "The Three Comings are part of the cosmic design. They can't be stopped. They *will* happen. But the Second Coming—this current stage—is humanity's responsibility. It's up to humans to prepare themselves for the Third Coming."

"Prepare how?" I ask.

"By resisting temptation," E answers. "By refusing corruption. By choosing compassion, faith, and hope, even in the face of darkness." He gestures toward me, his gaze unwavering. "And that's where you come in, Isabella. Your actions, your choices, are more important than you realize. They ripple outward, affecting not just this realm, but all realms."

My mouth goes dry, letting his words settle. "What does any of this have to do with me?"

A's gaze softens. "When you tried to take your own life, you disrupted the balance between life and death. That act caused a fracture in the veil—a crack that exposed the Seven Seals. It's not just your own soul at stake anymore, Isabella. It's the fate of countless others."

My heart races as memories of the dream flood back—souls being pulled into pits of fire, creatures crawling out of them, waiting at my feet. My stomach knots, realizing that the dream had meaning. My dreams have been trying to tell me something, and I haven't been listening.

"The Seven Seals?" I ask, shaken.

"They're cosmic markers," A explains, her tone solemn. "Each seal represents a phase of humanity's transformation—Conquest, War, Famine, Death, and so on. They were designed to break gradually over millennia, guiding humanity toward the fulfillment of the divine plan. But your actions have caused the timeline to shift. The angels of death want to use this disruption to break the seals prematurely."

E's expression hardens. "They want to force the Third Coming before humanity is ready. They've lost faith in the world and want to bring about the Final Judgment now, regardless of the cost."

"Why me?" I rasp, my voice trembling. "Why do they think I'm the key?"

A's gaze sharpens. "There's an ancient prophecy—one that speaks of a human born in a time when the love for God has dimmed, when sin and corruption consume the world. This person will lead humanity down one of two paths: redemption or destruction. They hold the power to bridge the realms, to either restore balance or shatter what remains of it. But their role is not to bring final judgment—only to prepare humanity for it. And we believe that person is you, Isabella."

The words hit me like a blow, knocking the air from my lungs. My head spins, my pulse pounding in my ears. "So… what exactly am I supposed to do? Save the world?"

"Not just the world," E says, his voice low but resolute. "All worlds. All realms. The balance of existence depends on you staying on the right path."

"And if I don't?" I manage to ask.

A's expression darkens. "If you don't, the Sixth Seal will bring disasters beyond imagination. And the Seventh Seal

"…" She pauses, letting her words sink in. "That will mark the end of everything."

A wave of fear washes over me, my breath catching in my throat.

"You're stronger than you think, Isabella," E adds, urgency creeping into his tone. "But the angels of death are masters of manipulation. They'll use your grief, your fear, your love for Julian—anything they can—to sway you."

I squeeze Julian's hand tighter, the warmth grounding me amidst the chaos of their words. "And Julian? Why can I interact with him outside of dreams but only see you two in them?"

A and E exchange a glance, hesitation flickering between them.

"There's still so much you don't know, isn't there?" My voice comes out sharper than I intended. "Why don't you just ask God? Don't you answer to the Big Man—or Big Woman?"

Another glance passes between them, unease crossing their faces

"Nobody has seen or heard from God in …" E trails off, frustration flashing in his expression. He shakes his head. "You know what? We need ground rules. No questions about God or Jesus. No existential questions."

I blink, dumbfounded. "What's the fun in that?" The words tumble out before I can stop them.

"We're also not supposed to be having this conversation," A says. "Nor are you supposed to know how we look."

I sigh, understanding what they're saying. "Touché."

Finally, A answers. "We don't fully understand your connection to Julian. But it's clear your bond with him is strong—so strong that it defies the natural order."

I look up at Julian, my heart aching. "Then why was he taken from me in the first place?"

Silence falls, thick and heavy with unspoken truths.

A steps forward, her tone softening. "You've been given a lot to process, Isabella. Take your time to understand your role in this. But know this—you are not alone."

E nods, his earlier edge diminished. "We'll be here to guide you. But in the end, the choices are yours. What happens next depends on you."

I nod, though my thoughts whirl in a storm of confusion and doubt.

The air around us begins to shimmer, the edges of the realm blurring. Shadows unfurl and curl back into themselves, the scene wavering between reality and dream. I close my eyes, letting the distortion carry me away.

CHAPTER 32

I wake up to the sound of voices and laughter drifting up from downstairs. For a moment, I lie still, staring at the ceiling. My room looks the same. Feels the same. Everything around me seems normal.

But I know it isn't. Not after last night.

I can talk to my guardian angels. Julian was real—I didn't imagine him. And now, apparently, the fate of everything rests in my hands.

No big deal. Just another Saturday morning.

There's a knock at my door, and Sara walks in before I can respond.

"Oh good, you're awake. Tía Lupe and Tía Sofía are here," she announces.

"What? Why? Isn't it too early for visitors?" I mutter, sitting up and rubbing my face.

"Elle, it's almost noon. And did you forget we invited the family over for lunch today?"

I groan. Right. The lovely lunch Sara had planned. I had completely forgotten that she invited the aunts over today. Of course, it had to be *today* of all days.

Funny timing, God. How am I supposed to process *everything* at this rate? This wasn't a dream, right?

No.

The word cuts sharply into my thoughts, the voice unmistakable. A.

A chill runs down my spine. Okay. It's all real. Got it.

"¡Ándale! Shower and come downstairs—we need your help setting up," Sara says, her tone edged with impatience before disappearing through the door.

I sit there for a moment longer, staring after her. My heart is pounding, my mind racing. I feel like I'm being pulled in two directions—half of me desperate to cling to normalcy, the other half consumed by everything I now know.

Finally, I pull myself out of bed. One thing at a time. Shower first. Then I can deal with angels, Julian, and the literal fate of the universe later.

After I shower, I head downstairs. The house is alive with laughter and chatter. It's been months since we've had family over, and though overwhelming, it feels surprisingly nice.

"Buenas tardes, mija," Tía Lupe says with a warm smile when she spots me.

"Buenas tardes," I reply, a bit awkwardly, nodding to her and everyone else.

I go around the room, greeting my aunts, their husbands, and my cousins.

"It's been a while, prima. ¿Cómo estás?" Juan, Tía Lupe's youngest son, says pulling me into a quick hug.

"I'm alright," I reply, offering a small smile.

After catching up with everyone—asking about my cousins who live in Mexico and listening to updates on family life—I join my sister and aunts in the kitchen to help while the men set up the canopy in the backyard.

The kitchen is chaotic, but in a good way. Pots and pans clatter, the smell of fresh tortillas and mole fills the air, and my aunts' voices overlap as they exchange recipes and swap the latest gossip.

"Elle, pass me that bowl," Sara says, waving me over.

"Which one?"

"The green one, with the salsa," she says, nodding toward the counter.

I hand it to her, and she pauses, giving me a quick glance. "You doing okay?"

I nod quickly. "Yeah, just taking it all in. It's nice."

Sara smiles warmly before turning back to what she was doing. I settle into the rhythm of helping—chopping vegetables, running cups of water outside, laughing at my aunts' occasional jokes.

It feels good. The normalcy of it all. Even though, deep down, I know it won't last.

By the time everyone leaves, it's 7:00 p.m. The house is quiet again, and exhaustion settles over the three of us as we crash onto the couch.

"Clean now or tomorrow?" Sara asks, eyeing the pile of dishes stacked in the kitchen.

I sigh, sinking deeper into the cushions. "Tomorrow," I mumble, swinging my legs onto Sara's lap and resting my head on Manny's shoulder.

"Ah, mírala," Sara teases. "Get comfy, why don't you." She shoves my legs off her lap with a playful smile.

I laugh—a genuine, unrestrained laugh. Manny, on the other hand, doesn't move. He lets me stay where I am, my head still resting on his shoulder.

"What do you guys say to a movie night?" he asks, breaking the silence. "There's plenty of leftover dessert from the aunts. We could snack while we watch."

"That's a good idea," Sara says, perking up. "But I get to pick the movie this time."

"Hey!" he protests, grinning. "You liked the last one."

"Not the point," she says, standing up to grab the leftover desserts.

I smile to myself, letting their playful bickering fill the space around me. For now, I let myself sink into this moment—the warmth of home, the laughter, the illusion of normalcy.

Because deep down, I know moments like this won't last forever.

CHAPTER 33

Lying in the darkness, I stare at Julian's photo on the nightstand, barely able to make out the details of his face.

I sigh and roll onto my back, eyes drifting to the ceiling. Today had been a welcome distraction, but now that it's over, I'm alone again—left with nothing but my thoughts.

"Julian," I whisper into the silence. "I need you."

At first, there's nothing. Just the stillness of the room.

But then, a familiar warmth slowly spreads through the air. The atmosphere shifts, something unseen stirring around me. My breath catches as I turn toward the window.

And there he is.

Standing by the window, bathed in the faint glow of the night, Julian watches me.

"Hi, Chave," he murmurs.

"Julian." Relief floods through me. Without thinking, I throw off the blankets and rush to him, nearly crashing into his arms. He holds me tightly, his embrace solid, real.

"I don't know what to do," I whisper against his chest, my voice breaking. "Everything is overwhelming."

"I know it's a lot, amor," he says gently.

My heart skips a beat at the sound of him calling me *amor*. For a brief second, the seriousness of everything fades away.

How this is even real—how Julian is standing here in our room, holding me as though he never left—feels incomprehensible. If I ever tried explaining this to anyone, they'd think I've finally lost my mind to grief.

After a long moment, I pull back to look at him properly, desperate to take in every detail of his face.

But it's too dark.

I untangle myself from his arms, walk to the nightstand, and turn on the lamp. A soft glow spills across the room, illuminating his face.

My breath catches. My heart skips.

Has he always been this handsome?

Julian was always good-looking, but now there's something different about him—a glow. His features are sharper, almost impossibly symmetrical.

Julian lets out a soft chuckle, teasing. "Chave, you're drooling."

"No, I'm not," I shoot back, heat rushing to my cheeks.

His laughter deepens as he closes the distance between us in a few easy steps. My pulse quickens, his presence overwhelming in the best—and strangest—way.

A nervous energy flutters through me—exhilarating and unnerving.

I feel alive.

He gently lifts my chin, tilting my face toward his as he leans in. I hold my breath, my lips parting slightly in anticipation. But instead of kissing me, he presses a soft, lingering kiss to my forehead.

Before I can even process the moment, Julian moves with a speed that leaves me breathless. In an instant, we're lying on the bed, facing each other.

My mind races, scrambling for a logical explanation for how this is even possible. But another part of me—the part that's longed for this—doesn't want logic.

I still don't understand how any of this works, but right now, it doesn't matter. I have him here, even if it's impossible. Even if I'm the only one who knows.

"What are you thinking?" Julian asks, his voice pulling me from my thoughts.

I hesitate for a moment, then smirk. "That I'm glad Sara isn't sleeping in here anymore because I'd have a lot of explaining to do."

He chuckles, the sound familiar. "Yeah, you would. Especially if you keep pulling me here."

I pause, my smile fading. "Wait." A flicker of confusion runs through me. "A and E said they don't really understand our connection. But you just said I'm pulling you here. How can you be so sure?"

His expression turns thoughtful. "I don't know exactly how to explain it. It's like… I can feel you reaching out for me. The more you need me, the stronger that pull gets. And then suddenly, I'm here—wherever you are."

I go quiet, absorbing his words. I hadn't realized I was calling to him—not intentionally, anyway.

"So you're saying I can just pull you from the other side? Whenever I want?" I ask, trying to wrap my head around it.

He gives a small shrug. "No estoy seguro. The best way to find out is to test it."

"And when you go back… what happens? What pulls you away?"

Julian's gaze softens. "You do. I think you're the one who decides how long I can stay. Like that day when Sara nearly walked in—you panicked, and I was pulled back."

I bite my lip, unsettled by the memory. His explanation only leaves me with more questions than answers. A new thought forms, something I hadn't considered before.

"But how do you know all this?" I ask, searching his face. "Have you told A and E? How much do they know?"

Julian frowns slightly, his brow furrowing as if trying to grasp something just beyond his reach. "I'm not entirely sure. It's strange—while we're talking, things are clicking into place. Like I'm realizing it alongside you."

He pauses, his gaze dropping for a moment before meeting mine again. "A and E believe it's … Well, they think it's God's way of speaking to us—spiritual beings."

His words linger in the air, heavy with meaning. I try to process it, but it feels too big—too divine—for me to fully grasp.

"God's way of talking …" I repeat softly, more to myself than to him.

Julian shifts lightly. "Chave, whatever happens, you're not alone," he says. "I know it feels like you are because you can't talk to anyone about this. But you can always talk to me."

I know he believes what he's saying, but I'm not sure I do. I want to—I really do—but all of this still feels unreal to fully accept.

Julian watches me for a moment before his expression softens, a playful glint flickering in his eyes. "Hey… do you remember our first date?" His voice is lighter now, teasing, a small smile tugging at his lips.

I let out a quiet chuckle. "Oh, I remember. Do *you*, though? Because you've always told a different version of what actually happened."

Julian laughs softly, and I soak in the sound, tucking it away in my memory.

"I took you to what we *thought* was a fancy restaurant back then because, you know, we were broke college students," he begins, his eyes dancing with amusement. "You wore that nice sundress you loved, and I was trying to look sharp in my best dark jeans and a button-up shirt."

"Okay … and then?" I ask, raising an eyebrow, prompting him to continue.

Julian tries to stifle his laughter. "You wanted dessert, but I didn't have enough money to pay for it. So I told the waitress it was your birthday—even though it *definitely* wasn't. They sang to you and brought out a free dessert."

He's laughing now, the memory bright in his eyes, and I can't help but grin too.

"Wow," I say, feigning shock. "You actually told it how it happened. I'm impressed."

My sarcasm only makes him laugh harder, his shoulders shaking with the effort. For a brief, perfect moment, it feels like nothing has changed—like we're just us, two people sharing a memory and teasing each other like we always used to.

We slip easily into talking about the past, our voices soft in the quiet of the room. He teases me about the early days, about the back-and-forth flirting that he thought was so obvious.

"I was practically throwing myself at you," he says, grinning.

"Please," I scoff, laughing. "You were not that smooth. And I wasn't oblivious—I just didn't think you'd ever go for me."

Julian shakes his head, still smiling. "Chave, I was giving you every sign in the world. I couldn't have been more obvious if I'd written it on a billboard."

I laugh, unable to argue, and he chuckles, reminding me of all the ways he tried to get my attention. There were subtle and not-so-subtle hints that flew right over my head.

From there, the conversation flows effortlessly, like slipping into an old rhythm we never lost. We talk about our friends, our inside jokes, the little things only we would understand. We revisit all our *firsts*—the first time we held hands, our first kiss, the first time he told me he loved me.

And finally, we talk about our wedding day.

I tell him how nervous I was, how I was certain I'd trip walking down the aisle. He admits he thought he might pass out from nerves, his palms sweating, his heart racing.

I remember the moment I saw him waiting at the end of the aisle—how everything else faded, how my world narrowed to him alone. A big smile had spread across my face, and I'll never forget the way his eyes filled with tears when he saw me in my dress for the first time. That look in his eyes had been everything—love, promise, the future we were building together.

Time melts away as we lie there, facing each other, lost in our most precious memories. His hand rests between us, close enough to touch. I reach out, lacing my fingers through his.

The warmth of his hand reminds me of everything we were, everything we had. The ache in my chest eases, giving way to something gentler—a feeling of peace.

I feel whole.

CHAPTER 34

I don't remember falling asleep. The last thing I remember was staring into Julian's brown eyes, feeling his hand warm in mine. But now, I wake up alone in my room. Julian is gone.

A hollow ache settles in my chest, a familiar reminder of his absence.

I must have sent him back the moment I drifted off.

Rolling onto my side, I reach for my phone on the nightstand. The screen reads 11:11 AM, the numbers tugging at something in the back of my mind. *Isn't 1111 an angelic number?* I try to remember the meaning, but I can't quite remember.

What I do know is that I feel rested, for once. There were no dreams, no restless tossing and turning—just deep, uninterrupted sleep. And it feels good.

I can hear movement downstairs and the faint sound of clinking dishes.

Throwing the blankets to the side, I climb out of bed and open my door. I'm immediately greeted by the rich aroma of coffee drifting up the stairs, making my mouth water.

When I walk into the kitchen, Sara is pouring herself a cup of coffee while Manny rummages through the fridge.

"Morning," I say, sliding into a chair at the kitchen table.

"Morning," Sara replies, holding up the coffee pot. "Coffee?"

"Sí, por favor," I say with a nod as I wrap my hands around the warmth of the mug she sets in front of me a moment later.

"Morning," Manny finally greets, his head still halfway inside the refrigerator. "Any preference on breakfast?"

"Not really," Sara and I say at the same time.

"Good," Manny says, emerging with an assortment of ingredients and setting them on the counter. "Because there's not much left. We've got exactly enough eggs to make huevos a la Mexicana."

"My favorite," I say, taking a sip of coffee.

Sara takes a seat beside me, curling her hands around her mug. "Since we missed the 10:00 a.m. Mass, are we going to the 12:30 p.m. one?" she asks, looking at Manny.

Manny glances up from chopping a tomato. "Um... Elle, what do you think? Go to Mass or buy groceries? We're low on basically everything."

"Why are you making me decide?" I ask, a flicker of annoyance creeping into my tone.

"Let's skip for today," Sara says, stepping in quickly.

Manny glances up, clearly relieved. "Works for me. After breakfast, do you guys want to come with me to the grocery store?"

"Sure," I say without thinking. The word surprises me the moment it leaves my mouth—and judging by the way Manny and Sara both stare at me, it surprises them too.

Sara shoots Manny a quick look, half-surprised, half-amused. It takes me a second to understand why. This is probably the first time I've voluntarily agreed to go out—outside of family events, Mass, therapy, or my recent morning walks.

"So, groceries after breakfast?" I ask, deliberately ignoring their exchanged glance.

"Yup!" Sara replies, her grin wide.

I smile faintly into my coffee, then glance at her. "By the way, Sara, is there someone new in your life? You've been texting a lot lately … and taking a bunch of calls in secret."

Her fingers freeze mid-motion, gripping the rim of her mug. "What? No," she mumbles, her voice unusually small.

I raise an eyebrow. "So …"

Sara exhales, long and slow, and avoids our gazes. "It's Joe."

I blink. Manny looks just as surprised as I feel.

Joe is her ex-boyfriend.

A wave of guilt spreads through me. I never asked her what really happened between them. Never checked in to see how she was doing. *How did I miss this?*

The realization sinks deep, curling in my stomach. I've been so consumed by my own struggles that I haven't even thought to ask Sara about him—or about *anything*, really. And now, for the first time since everything, she's bringing him up.

"Sorry," she says quietly, fiddling with the handle of her mug. "I didn't mean to—"

"Don't apologize," I interrupt, offering her a warm smile. "Really. I want to know what's going on with you, Sara. I've missed everything. I'm sorry."

She glances up at me, surprise flickering in her eyes, before a small, grateful smile tugs at her lips.

"It's okay, Elle. You're here now."

It does feel like I'm here now. Not just physically, but really here, living in the present with my family instead of being trapped in the past.

"So … Does that mean you two are talking again?" Manny asks, sliding back into the conversation as he starts chopping an onion.

Sara sighs, her gaze dropping to her coffee as she traces a finger along the rim of her mug. "Yeah. Joe's been texting me. Apologizing. Saying he misses me."

As she talks, the pieces begin to fall into place.

She tells us how Joe felt neglected because she was spending so much time helping me. How he gave her an ultimatum—him or her family. And, of course, she chose us.

My stomach twists. *I should've known this sooner. I should've asked.*

I glance at Manny, searching for his reaction. But his knife doesn't pause.

He already knew.

Hearing this makes something twist in my chest, hot and sharp. Anger rises at the thought of someone who claimed to love her putting her in that position. If he couldn't stand by her during one of the hardest times of our lives, then he has no right to stand by her now.

"Sara," I say as calmly as possible. "It's your life and your choice if you want to give Joe another chance. But the way he reacted back then … It says a lot about him. I think you're better off without him."

Sara and Manny both stare at me like I've just grown a third head. I'm not sure if they're surprised we're having this conversation at all—or if it's the fact that I'm actually present enough to be giving advice.

Sara's lips curve into a small smile, and lets out a soft laugh. "Since when did you get so wise, Elle?"

I shrug, feeling a little self-conscious but also… proud. "No sé. Ahora veo las cosas un poco diferente."

Manny chuckles, shaking his head as he stirs the pan on the stove.

As breakfast finishes cooking, the conversation flows naturally. Sara talks through her dilemma, and by the time Manny slides a plate of eggs and tortillas in front of me, she exhales deeply, as if finally settling into her decision.

"I think you're right," she says firmly. "I deserve someone who doesn't put conditions on me."

"Claro que sí," Manny says with a grin as he takes a seat at the table

I smile, a rare sense of ease settling over me. As we start eating, I glance at Manny with a smirk. "Speaking of people… whatever happened with—what was her name again?"

"Monica," Sara chimes in with a smirk, clearly delighted to shift the attention to him.

Oh, right—Monica. The woman Manny always claimed he wasn't interested in, until she finally wore him down and convinced him to go on a date. They actually ended up going on a couple of dates, if I remember correctly.

Manny groans, running a hand through his hair. "No empiecen," he warns.

Sara and I burst into laughter, the sound warm and easy.

Manny tries to play it cool, but the red creeping up his neck betrays him. Unfortunately for him, his skin doesn't hide a blush the way mine does—one of the downsides of having lighter skin.

"There's nothing to say," he mutters, eyes locked on his plate as he grabs another tortilla, avoiding eye contact.

Sara and I exchange a knowing glance, grinning over our plates. But we decide to let him off hook.

Manny's shoulders relax slightly when he realizes we won't press any further.

For now.

But Sara and I both know we'll bring it up later—when he least expects it.

That's what sisters are for.

The conversation shifts to a grocery list and what we should do the remainder of the weekend.

I'm no longer going through the motions of life. I'm here.

CHAPTER 35

The Sunday afternoon heat is relentless. My phone says it's 95 degrees but feels like 103, and I believe it. I don't remember September ever being this unbearable. Even the short walk from the car to the grocery store leaves me sweating.

The moment we step inside, a rush of cool air washes over me, soothing my overheated skin. It feels so good.

Manny takes charge of the cart, wheeling it along as Sara and I wander through the aisles, grabbing items and tossing them in.

For a Sunday afternoon, the grocery store isn't as packed as it usually is, which is a pleasant surprise. I can actually enjoy looking at things without people crowding the aisles.

"Oh, I forgot to grab cookies," I say as we reach the second-to-last aisle before checkout. "I'll be right back."

I make my way back to the cookie aisle. The aisle is completely empty.

I stroll down the aisle looking at all choices. I stand in front of a few options while weighing which one would be better.

Then—a chill.

It creeps up the back of my neck, sharp and unnatural, sending a shiver down my spine.

From the corner of my eye, I see something.

A dark figure.

Standing at the far end of the aisle. Unmoving. Watching me.

My breath catches. My heart pounds as I turn abruptly—

Nothing.

Just the quiet hum of fluorescent lights overhead.

I shake it off, forcing myself to focus on the shelves again. But as I stare at the rows of cookies, there it is again. A shadow lingering just at the edge of my vision.

I whirl around a second time.

Nothing.

A prickle of fear crawls up my throat, my instincts screaming at me to *leave*. Without hesitation, I turn and walk in the opposite direction, my steps quick and unsteady.

I'm almost at the end of the aisle when I crash into someone.

I stumble back, a small gasp escaping my lips.

"¡Órale!" Sara exclaims, grabbing my shoulders to steady me. "I've been looking for you! We're about to pay. Where are the cookies?"

I blink at her and glance over my shoulder. The aisle is empty. There's no one there.

Right.

The cookies.

"Um, I decided not to get them," I mumble, gently prying Sara's hands off my shoulders.

She gives me a curious look but shrugs it off. "Okay, well, let's go before Mr. Grumpy-pants calls me," she says, rolling her eyes as she starts walking—straight down the very aisle I was trying to escape.

I hesitate for a moment, glancing back one last time. Nothing. Still, the unease lingers as I follow her, my heart beating faster than it should.

I instinctively reach for my black bracelet, my fingers brushing over the small cross. I rub it gently, and an immediate sense of comfort washes over me.

I'd forgotten how the bracelet has a way of giving me a sense of safety. As if, somehow, it's protecting me from unseen forces.

Cálmate, Elle, I tell myself. *You're seeing things that aren't there, and the bracelet is just a bracelet.*

But with everything I've been experiencing lately, I'm not sure I fully believe that anymore.

Later that night, I lie awake, staring at the ceiling, my mind heavy with questions.

There's so much I don't know. So much I don't understand.

Why me?

Why would God choose *me*—someone so flawed, so ordinary—to carry the faith of humanity in my hands? The thought is overwhelming. *It's insane.*

I've been avoiding these questions, refusing to let them linger long enough to spiral into a panic attack.

But I can't keep running from them.

Sooner or later, I'll have to face the truth. And it's starting to feel like sooner is coming faster than I'd hoped.

I need to talk to A and E.

Taking a deep breath, I close my eyes, silently willing my subconscious to know where to take me.

CHAPTER 36

When I open my eyes again, I'm greeted by the vivid colors and breathtaking beauty of the other realm. My subconscious really does know exactly where to take me.

Just a few feet away, A, E, and Julian are waiting.

The moment my gaze lands on Julian, my heart skips a beat. A smile tugs at my lips before I can stop it. Part of me wants to run to him, but I resist the urge, forcing myself to walk calmly toward the trio.

"Elle," A greets with a nod.

"Hi … again," I reply, my voice coming out awkward and unsure.

"Welcome back," E says with a relaxed smile, his tone warm and inviting.

I manage a small smile in return and instinctively move to Julian's side—where I feel most at ease. He takes my hand in a reassuring grip, his gentle smile steadying me.

"What can we do for you?" A asks, her presence as commanding as ever.

"Me?" I blink, caught off guard.

"You called us here," E explains, his tone calm and matter-of-fact.

"Oh." I say. *I can do that?*

"I see you're still figuring out how to use your … gift," A says knowingly, clearly picking up on my confusion.

"¿Tú crees?" I mutter sarcastically, unable to stop myself.

E lets out a low chuckle, and my face heats with embarrassment. *Seriously, Elle? Giving attitude to a divine being? Get it together.*

"Now this is the Elle we know," E teases, amusement clear in his voice.

Julian squeezes my hand gently. When I glance up at him, he's smiling—pleased. It's the same expression Sara and Manny gave me this morning, a quiet kind of joy, like he's relieved to see a glimpse of the old me shining through.

"Well, I guess I do have some questions that keep bothering me," I admit, turning my attention back to A and E.

No need for pleasantries. I'd rather get straight to the point—small talk has never really been my thing.

A and E watch me intently, their patience almost unnerving. But somehow, I get the distinct feeling they already know what I'm about to ask. After all, they're my guardian angels—don't they have access to my thoughts and feelings? Or is that not how this works?

"Don't worry, we can't read your thoughts. We're just really good at reading your body language. The only way we can hear your thoughts is if you allow us to," E explains, his tone calm but laced with that usual touch of mischief. "The only one who knows what you're thinking—and knows you better than you know yourself—is God. Of course, it's up to you how you choose to live."

"Well, that's a relief," I mumble under my breath, suddenly recalling all the embarrassing thoughts I've probably had. *Thank God they couldn't hear those.*

E's laugh erupts, deep and rich, filling the space around us. It's one of those full-bodied, chest-deep laughs that's warm and just a little teasing.

I freeze. *Am I making faces again?*

My expressions tend to betray my thoughts without me realizing it, and now I'm painfully aware of myself. *Great, Elle. Could you be more awkward? Get it together— you're here for answers, not a meltdown.*

E notices my embarrassment, and his laughter only grows. His eyes crinkle at the corners as he tries, and fails, to stifle it.

"Elle," he says between chuckles, his voice warm with amusement. "Forgive me. It's just … It's really good to see your old self again. It's good to have you back." His expression softens as he adds, "And please, talk to us like you would close friends or family."

A shoots him a pointed look, her lips pressed into a firm line. He shrugs, still grinning, clearly unbothered by her disapproval. He knows he's testing her patience—and he's enjoying every second of it.

Finally, A sighs and shakes her head, conceding. "He's right," she says, reluctant but sincere. "Just talk to us as if we were … well, like a friend or your siblings. We're here to help."

They're trying to make me feel comfortable, and I appreciate it. Maybe, just maybe, I'll stop being so awkward around my guardian angels for once.

"Anyway, as we were," A says, steering the conversation back on track, reminding me why I came in the first place.

I nod. "Right, anyway," I say, awkwardly.

"You guys said that I'm not alone and that you'll guide me down the right path. But how exactly?" I ask, the questions spilling out before I can stop them. "How are you going to protect me from the angels of death? Can they get to me? I don't understand how this is supposed to work."

The three of them exchange glances, a silent conversation passing between them, as if deciding who should take the lead.

After a moment, E is the one that speaks.

"Elle, we're always with you. You just haven't fully realized it yet," he says. "That gut feeling you sometimes get? Or those random thoughts that cross your mind— the ones that don't quite feel like your own? That's us, communicating with you. We've been protecting you for a long time. But now that you've come into your gift, you're more aware of us—and able to reach us more easily. That said …"

He pauses, his expression growing more serious. "You can't pull us into your realm like you do with Julian. Since we don't have a physical form, it's more difficult for us to appear on Earth."

I soak in his words, remembering the first time I heard A's voice in my head after coming here. It felt so surreal, but now it's starting to make sense.

"Does that mean you're fighting off the angels of death? Are they trying to reach me?"

A steps in. "It's true that it's been more challenging to shield you completely. The angels of death are allowed to walk the Earth, which means they can get close to you whenever they want. Our power only extends so far, and since we're not technically permitted on Earth ourselves, it's harder to keep them at bay. So, yes—they are trying very hard to reach you."

"However," E adds, his gaze flickering to my wrist, "your black bracelet—the one your grandmother gave you—it's been protecting you. When a loved one gifts you something like that, a religious article that's been blessed, it carries their love, their prayers, their intentions. That makes it powerful enough to shield you from supernatural beings, including the angels of death."

"Without it," E continues, "you'd be exposed to all sorts of things that linger on Earth. That bracelet has been shielding what you humans call your third eye."

I glance down at the bracelet, running my fingers over the smooth knots.

"So if I took it off, I'd be vulnerable?" I ask, my voice quiet but steady.

A nods firmly. "Yes. Removing it would open you up—not just to the angels of death, but to everything else."

The wheels in my head start turning, piecing together everything they're telling me. This bracelet, something I've worn without a second thought since my grandma sent it to me, has been protecting me in ways I never could have imagined.

"Is there a way to close my 'third eye' completely?" I ask. "Like … permanently?"

E's expression turns cautious. He rubs the back of his neck and glances at A before finally answering. "No," he says, his tone slow and deliberate, carefully weighing each word. "Once that door is open, you can never close it completely. You can shield yourself from the supernatural—but not always."

Shield myself? What does that even mean?

E watches me in silence, his eyes unreadable. But beneath it, there's something else—something unspoken. Something that twists my stomach.

"We sensed you were different from any other human, but we never imagined you'd be the one tied to the rumored prophecy."

My mind is racing.

"There are humans who are sensitive to the supernatural," he continues, his tone measured. "Some are more attuned than others. You're on the far end of that spectrum."

He pauses, letting the words sink in. "Do you remember the first apartment you, Sara, and Manny moved into after your parents passed? You kept sensing your parents there. You could feel their touch."

The memory rushes back, sharp and vivid. I had forgotten about it—or maybe buried it.

I remember sitting on the couch late at night, feeling the warmth of hands brushing my shoulder, hearing whispers that sounded like my parents telling me it would be okay.

I kept telling Sara and Manny that Mom and Dad were checking in on us.

But Sara—she snapped.

"If they're really here, why can't I feel them too?" she'd shouted, her voice cracking with grief.

She was right to be angry. We were all grieving.

And just like that, I stopped sensing my parents. They faded away. But somehow, I knew they were happy. I knew we'd eventually be okay.

Other moments throughout my life flicker in my mind—times when I heard, sensed, or even *saw* things no one else could. But I had always blamed it on my imagination.

"It wasn't your imagination," A says. "And as we've mentioned before, once that door has been opened it cannot be closed, as far as we know. All we can do is try to protect you."

She pauses, choosing her words carefully. "What we *do* know is that your gift is growing. We'll keep learning alongside you, as God intends."

Her tone shifts, turning more serious. "We're also aware that the angels of death have been lurking. You've always been sensitive to their presence, which is why you can *feel* them watching you. But as long as you keep your bracelet on, it will be difficult for them to break through the barriers protecting you. For now, all they can do is let you sense them."

I take a slow breath, letting it all sink in.

The more answers I get, the more questions I have.

My head spins with everything I'm learning, but at least I'm starting to understand the mess I've found myself in.

"Chave, I think that's enough questions for one visit," Julian says, finally speaking up. He's been quiet by my side, letting A and E do most of the talking. "You can come back whenever you need to, but I think you've been overloaded. You need to rest now."

"We agree," E adds. "And remember, you can always reach out to us, even when you're awake. Just pay closer attention, and you'll hear us."

I squeeze Julian's hand, nodding. "Okay, I'll try. So, just to make sure I've got this straight ... I need to keep my bracelet on at all times, no matter what. Trust my instincts. And stay on guard."

A nods. "Yes. For now, that's all you need to focus on. You've been doing great so far, despite everything. We're proud of you. And remember, Elle—you're not alone."

"I'll try," I say.

The realm around me begins to blur, the colors fading as I feel the familiar pull back to my realm. Julian's hand slips from mine, but before he lets go, he gives me one last reassuring squeeze.

CHAPTER 37

When I wake up the next morning, it's already 8:45 a.m. There's so much I need to process after last night's visit to the other realm, but one step at a time.

I stretch, climb out of bed, and start getting ready for my morning walk. It's Monday, so Manny and Sara have already left for work.

I've purposely chosen weekday mornings for my walks—when the neighborhood is at its quietest. Most people are at work, kids are in school, and the few stay-at-home moms don't usually come outside until later. This way, I get the neighborhood pretty much all to myself.

As I step outside, the warm morning air fills my lungs, but my mind is elsewhere. I replay everything A and E told me. A and E answered so many of my questions, but now new ones are bubbling up.

Like … How exactly am I going to save humanity? Stay on the right path, but what does that look like? I know E had listed a few things but I need something more concrete. Examples. A real plan.

I let out a slow sigh.

Suddenly, a familiar cold chill creeps up the back of my neck, sending a shiver through me despite the warmth of the sun.

The sensation is unmistakable—something is watching me, following me. My heart quickens as I whirl around, scanning the empty street. But there's nothing there.

In the distance, I hear the faint sound of a crying baby. I also notice something else. The birds, which had been chirping moments ago, have gone silent.

The uneasy stillness wraps around me, and I can't shake the feeling that I'm no longer alone.

I have the urge to run, but I stand my ground.

"Whatever you are, go away. Leave me alone," I say to whatever is out there that I can't see.

Within seconds, the sound of chirping returns, and the eerie sensation of being watched fades away.

Deciding I've had enough walking for the day, I turn around and head back home.

Once inside, I sink onto the couch, letting out a long breath as I try to shake off the lingering unease. I close my eyes, take a few deep breaths, and rest my head against the back of the couch, trying to make myself relax.

And then—

Everything shifts.

I'm sitting at my childhood kitchen table, back in my old home. My mom and dad are across from me, laughing, their eyes bright and warm. It takes me a second to notice that Manny and Sara are sitting on either side of me—both younger. We're playing lotería, and the table is scattered with colorful cards and pinto beans.

"No, yo dije lotería primero. ¡Maaa!" Sara exclaims.

"Nah uh! Yo lo dije primero!" Manny argues, leaning forward, his face scrunched up in determination.

I join my parents in their laughter, the sound filling me with a warmth I haven't felt in ages. It's so good to be home. I missed my parents more than I can put into words.

"Ya, ya. Yo los escuché a los dos al mismo tiempo," my dad says, grinning as he looks at me. "Bella, ¿qué dices tú?"

My heart aches at the sound of that nickname—*Bella*. I haven't heard it since he passed away. Only my mom and dad ever called me that.

"M-M-M-M-Manny!" I say, dragging it out playfully.

Sara huffs and crosses her arms, pretending to be upset. "You always choose him," she says, shooting me an exaggerated glare.

But then everything changes. Now, I'm standing in the middle of a dark road, the smell of gasoline and burnt rubber thick in the air. Two cars sit twisted and mangled in front of me. My stomach drops as I recognize one of them. It's our family car.

Panicked whimpers come from somewhere nearby, and I start running, heart pounding as I scan the wreckage. That's when I see her—my mother, lying a few feet from the car. I drop to my knees beside her, my hands shaking as I take in the blood covering her face, her clothes. She's breathing, but barely.

"Bella?" she whispers, wincing as she struggles to focus on me. Hearing her say my name makes my chest tighten, the anxiety clawing its way up my throat. I don't know what to do. I don't know how to help her.

"¿Qué hago, mamá?" I ask, my voice trembling as I scan her injuries, unsure if I should touch her, unsure if I might make it worse.

She looks at me, her eyes heavy with pain. "Tu papá, mija … tu papá…" Her eyelids flutter, starting to close.

"Mamá! ¡Mamá!" Panic wells up inside me, but I force myself to look around, desperate to find my dad.

"Dad!" I scream, my voice breaking as I search the wreckage. "¡Papá!"

Then I hear it—a faint, broken voice calling my name. "Bella?"

It's my dad, his voice coming from somewhere within the twisted metal. I turn, my heart shattering as I realize he's trapped.

I start running toward him, but just before I reach the car, there's a sudden, blinding flash—and an explosion. The blast sends me flying backward, and I brace myself for impact… but it never comes.

When I open my eyes, I'm standing in a cold, sterile operating room. The air is thick with the sharp smell of antiseptic, and machines are shrieking, alarms going off all around me. My heart races as I take in the doctors and nurses swarming around the operating table, moving frantically, their faces tense.

I push through the crowd, desperate to see who's lying on the table. And then I see him.

"Julian!" I gasp, rushing to his side. He's pale, lifeless, his body still as the doctor performs chest compressions, shouting commands that blur into an overwhelming hum.

"Do something! Save him!" I scream at the doctor, grabbing his arm, but he doesn't respond. It's like I'm invisible, my words lost in the chaos.

I turn to Julian, tears streaming down my face as I reach for his hand, but it's already growing cold.

"No me hagas esto, Julian! ¡No me dejes!" I plead, my voice breaking as I clutch his hand, desperately willing him to hold on. But the machine lets out a steady, unbroken tone—the flatline.

"No … Diosito, no! Por favor, no!" I scream, raw and desperate.

A guttural, excruciating cry rips from my throat, shattering the silence of the room.

"Dios no te va a ayudar," says a voice from the shadows.

A figure begins to emerge from the darkness—a skeletal shape, shrouded in shadow, its face hidden.

La Muerte.

I stumble back, pressing against the cold edge of the operating table, my heartbeat pounds in my ears as the figure draws closer.

"Isabella," it says, its voice hollow, reverberating through the air, "life isn't fair. God takes the people you love most. Like your parents, Julian. For what? To test your faith?"

It lets out a low, mocking laugh.

"Humans are corrupt. They will never learn. They will never become what God believes they can be. Compassionate, good … worthy."

Its words seep into me, dark and venomous, and I feel my chest tighten with each one.

"So, Isabella," it continues, a cruel smile in its voice, "give in to that anger simmering inside you. You're allowed to be angry at God. After all, He took the people you loved the most… and left you completely alone."

My breath shudders. "I'm not alone," I say, my voice trembling as tears stream down my face.

But even as I say it, I feel the anger rising within me, hot and undeniable, spreading through my chest like fire.

La Muerte steps closer, the stench of decay filling the air.

"No?" It sneers, leaning in. "Dime, ¿dónde están tus ángeles de la guarda? Julian?"

At the mention of Julian, my gaze drops to the table. His lifeless body lies there, pale and still.

Pain claws at my throat.

He's gone.

My parents are gone. Julian is gone.

But then, another thought pushes through the haze. I have Sara and Manny. I have A. E. And Julian.

This is just a dream. La Muerte can't reach me here. The realization sends a spark of strength through me.

I lift my chin, stepping forward.

"No, you're wrong," I say, my voice steadying. "I'm not alone. And you have no power here."

As I speak the final words, the dream begins to unravel, the darkness around me crumbling into fragments.

I jolt awake, alone in the living room. I instinctively wrap my fingers around the knotted black cross on my bracelet.

They're closer than we thought.

The thought appears out of nowhere, clear and sharp. It's either A or E communicating with me.

A cold shiver crawls down my spine.

So it begins.

CHAPTER 38

I'm already twirling my wedding ring, even before Dr. Rivera asks her first question. She notices immediately.

The dream I had a few days ago left me rattled. The image of Julian lying lifeless on the operating table refuses to fade, playing over and over in my mind. Even though it was just a dream, seeing him like that was unbearable.

I need to get a grip on my emotions before I see Julian again. The dream stirred up feelings I thought I had already worked through, and I can't afford to fall apart in front of him. Not when there are bigger things at stake.

Then there's A and E who have been trying to communicate with me, but I've been pushing them away. I've also been careful not to pull Julian into this realm.

I take a deep breath. "I had a dream about my parents and Julian," I admit, my voice quieter than I intended.

"What happened in the dream?" Dr. Rivera asks, encouraging conversation.

I hesitate, then begin recounting it, my fingers still absentmindedly twisting my ring. Dr. Rivera listens intently, nodding here and there, occasionally jotting notes in her notebook.

I finish recounting the dream, making sure I leave out the part where La Muerte appeared. I can't tell her about La Muerte. I can't tell anyone. That part of the dream is my burden to carry, mine alone.

Dr. Rivera sets her pen down and looks at me thoughtfully.

"Let me ask you something," she says.

I tense slightly, wary of what she's about to ask. "Okay," I reply, bracing myself.

She studies me carefully. "Isabella, do you find yourself hiding or minimizing your grief from your siblings?"

The question catches me off guard. My fingers freeze, and I look up at her. Her words hit a nerve, stirring something I hadn't allowed myself to really think about before.

"Um … yes," I admit, my voice hesitant.

I pause, then continue, the words spilling out slowly, carefully. "Ever since my attempt … I feel like I have to hide how deep my grief really goes. I already feel like a burden to them. They've adjusted their entire lives for me, to help me, and …" I trail off.

"Isabella, you are not a burden to your siblings, nor should you feel guilty. From the way you've described them, they love you deeply. Supporting you is not something they've done out of obligation—it's something they've done because they care and want the best for you."

I glance down at my hands, twisting my wedding ring between my fingers. "But it's hard not to feel like I'm dragging them down. Manny and Sara have their own lives, their own things to worry about, and here I am … taking up space, disrupting everything."

Dr. Rivera leans forward slightly. "Taking up space is not a bad thing, Isabella. You are allowed to take up space. You're allowed to need help. Grief is heavy, and it's okay to lean on others to carry it with you. That doesn't make you a burden—it makes you human."

"But … I don't want them to worry about me anymore. They've already been through so much," I say faintly.

"I understand that," Dr. Rivera says softly. "But shutting them out doesn't protect them. It only builds distance. Sharing how you feel—being honest about your grief—doesn't mean you're putting the entire weight on them. It means you're letting them walk beside you through it."

I feel tears pricking the corners of my eyes, but I blink them away. I know she's right. I've spent so much time trying to shield Manny and Sara from my pain, thinking it was the right thing to do.

"And how would I do that?" I ask her.

Dr. Rivera offers a small, encouraging smile. "Start with something simple. A conversation. Let them know how much you appreciate their support. Then start with small steps and build from there."

I nod slowly, "Okay … I'll try."

"That's all I ask," she says gently.

I leave my session feeling more at ease. Although, Dr. Rivera didn't dive too much into my dreams and asked further questions. But she did ask a question that I hadn't let myself think too much about. But thanks to that, now I feel ready to talk to A, E, and Julian.

There are bigger things to face, and they can't wait any longer.

CHAPTER 39

I find myself staring up at the same ceiling I've been staring at more and more lately. It hasn't changed since last night. Except tonight, the room is pitch black, with no full moon to illuminate the shadows.

I close my eyes, and within moments, I'm transported to the other realm. It's starting to get easier. Julian was right. I just need to trust myself.

When I arrive, I see A, E, and Julian beneath a silver-leafed tree, its branches glowing softly with an ethereal light. They look up as I approach, their faces a mix of warmth and expectation—like they've been waiting for me.

"Took you long enough," E says, trying to keep the atmosphere light.

I glance at Julian. He watches me with an intensity that makes my chest tighten, like he can see right through the mask I'm barely holding in place. I swallow hard, pushing back the memory of his lifeless body on the operating table. He doesn't say a word.

"I'm sorry. I just needed time," I say, forcing myself to look away from Julian. I turn to A, who sits in silence, studying me with patience.

I lower myself to the ground between A and E, across from Julian.

"That's understandable," A says softly. "After all, we couldn't protect you from the angels of death. We told you we could, but we failed."

She's right. The angels of death broke through the protective barriers—the very ones that were supposed to keep them out.

"So why were they able to get through?" I ask. "I was the one who got myself out of that nightmare. Me." Bitterness laces my words.

How am I supposed to depend on them if they can't even keep me safe?

E's expression darkens. "They're growing stronger, and we don't know why. It's been difficult to gather information. Some of them still remain loyal to their duties, but they refuse to speak out. They're afraid to go against their leader. And since we can't break through their communication, predicting their next move has been impossible. We're trying to convince the ones who are still loyal to talk before they're forced to join the rebellion."

My stomach twists. "What do you mean by forced?"

"Besides the archangels, only the angels of death can cross between realms. Their main role is guiding souls to purgatory to await judgment. Because of this, God granted them their own way of communicating." E continues.

I blink. "Wait—you're telling me purgatory is real? I thought it was just some in-between place where souls got stuck?" The revelation catches me completely off guard. "And what does that have to do with them getting stronger?"

"Purgatory isn't what humans think it is," E says, shaking his head. "It's not a place to fear. Think of it more like … a waiting room. Souls stay there, awaiting judgment—whether that means being reborn to atone for past life debts or moving on to the final judgment." He stops abruptly, catching himself. "Hold on. We agreed—no existential questions."

I cross my arms. "Fine. But that still doesn't answer my question—why are the angels of death getting stronger?"

A picks up where E left off. "We believe that the more angels of death who join the rebellion, the more power they accumulate. It's like combining all their strength. And with that much power, even we can't stop them."

Julian scoffs, clearly irritated. "They should be answering to God, not taking power for themselves."

"Ok, but if God is all-knowing, He must have foreseen this rebellion. So why would He allow it?" I ask, frustration starting to edge into my voice.

A sighs, exasperated, as if she's explaining the simplest concept to a child. "Yes, God is all-knowing. He likely saw this coming. But there is always a reason for what He does," she says firmly.

"So why don't you question it?" I ask, my voice rising as my frustration bubbles over. "Why would He let any of this happen? Why would He put me in this situation?"

I know I'm being emotional, but after what I've been through—being forced to relive the deaths of the people I loved most—how do they expect me not to be? Aren't I allowed to ask questions? Aren't I allowed to be angry at Him for letting this happen?

"You're right," E says quietly. "Unlike us, humans were given free will. And with that free will comes the choice to question, to challenge, to even push God away."

"So you're telling me you'll always blindly trust Him?" I ask, feeling a pang of disbelief.

A's gaze grows tender as she responds. "Elle, we understand your frustration. But unlike humans, we were created without sin, and we existed long before humanity. Humans chose this path when they defied God. I'm not saying it's your fault that you're in this situation. But God has never abandoned you or us, even if it feels that way. It's humans who abandon Him. We're here to guide you toward the right path that God would like you to take, but ultimately, it's your choice whether to follow that path."

I clench my jaw, inhaling deeply through my nose. I understand what they're saying. I do. But the frustration still burns inside me, clouding my rationality. I just don't understand why God can't simply give us answers. If He allowed this rebellion, shouldn't He at least tell us how to stop it?

"Chave," Julian says finally, breaking the silence. I meet his gaze, but I have to look away almost immediately, the memory of his lifeless body flashing in my mind. "What did they want?"

"I'm not sure," I reply. "They showed me a happy memory … and then tore it away by forcing me to relive the two worst moments of my life." My eyes flicker toward Julian, but I quickly look away again, unable to hold his gaze.

Julian moves closer, his hand finding mine, his warmth grounding me, steadying me. I close my eyes, drawing in a slow breath, trying to push past the storm raging inside me.

"That doesn't tell us much," E says, rubbing his jaw in thought. "We'll have to investigate further. The only ones who might know more are the archangels, but they've been called to Earth to protect key portals. Communication with them is extremely limited."

"Portals?" I ask, frowning but intrigued.

A nods. "Portals allow supernatural beings to cross between realms. Their locations are highly classified. If something crosses over, it's usually because someone found a portal by chance. The angels of death are supposed to guard them, but with everything that's happening, they'll likely try to use the portals to their advantage. The archangels are trying to prevent that."

My breath catches. "¿Me estás diciendo que ya empezó todo?" I ask, the frustration I'd felt giving way to worry. "So what does that mean for me? Is my bracelet strong enough to protect me from the angels of death—from La Muerte?"

A hesitates, her expression cautious. "Elle, your bracelet is the most powerful tool you have. As long as you keep it on, it will protect you. But … there are limits."

My stomach tightens. "Limits?"

E nods, his expression darkening. "Dreams are unique in that they exist between realms. While you have more power in your dreams, we can usually enter them as well— to send messages, provide guidance, or even protect you. In your case, we would have entered your dream to shield you. But this time, something was blocking us. It felt like a barrier—a force we couldn't break through."

"A barrier?" I ask, frustration bubbling again. "If you're supposed to protect me, why couldn't you break through it? And now that I'm thinking about it, why haven't you entered my dreams when La Muerte showed up before?"

A glances at E, an unspoken exchange passing between them. There's hesitation there—reluctance.

"We didn't realize La Muerte had been slipping into your dreams." A finally says, her voice measured. "It seems it has been more meticulous than we thought. We only recently discovered that it was La Muerte was behind what influenced you to try and take your own life."

My mind spins her words sink in, and I'm hit with memories of the nightmares that left me feeling like Julian's death was my fault. The ones that made me believe I was a burden to my siblings. The ones that convinced me it should've been me instead.

My mind spins as memories rush back. The nightmares, the overwhelming guilt, the whispering voice in the dark telling me that Julian's death was my fault. The same voice that made me believe I was a burden. That convinced me I didn't deserve to be here.

It feels like a punch to the gut, knocking the air from my lungs.

"So it's been La Muerte this whole time?" I ask as the pieces start to fall into place.

A and E exchange another look, and this time, it's different. There's something deeper in their expression—something like guilt.

They're hiding something.

My pulse quickens. "What is it?" I demand, leaning closer, the storm in my chest swelling. "Tell me."

E hesitates before speaking, his tone cautious. "It seems La Muerte was also responsible for Julian's accident. That's why he became your spirit guide—because it wasn't his time yet. There was still more he needed to do. But we couldn't figure out what had caused his life to be cut short until recently."

His words barely register before the anger explodes inside me, white-hot and uncontrollable.

"Are you kidding me? ¡¿Qué chingados me estás diciendo?!" I snap, my anger boiling over, spilling out before I can stop it. I scramble to my feet.

"Chave, cálmate," Julian says, standing and stepping closer, reaching for my hand.

But I yank it away before he can touch me. "No, Julian, I will not calm down!" I snap, my voice breaking as the words spill out. "All of this is happening because of me! You died because of me—because that asshole, La Muerte, wants me to bring about the end of the realms. And what better way to push me onto the wrong path than by taking the love of my life from me? By making me angry at God, making me think it was His doing!"

Tears sting my eyes, blurring my vision as I choke out the words. My chest feels like it's caving in, crushed beneath the truth I can't escape.

In the end, La Muerte was right. It *is* my fault that Julian died.

If God had never made me "special," if I wasn't meant to fulfill some ancient prophecy, Julian would still be alive. He wouldn't have been taken. This is all my fault.

"Don't talk like that," Julian says, his voice filled with pain. He steps toward me again, reaching for my hand, but I take another step back, keeping the distance between us.

"It's not your fault, Isabella," A says firmly, her tone gentle.

I let out a sharp, bitter laugh. "And how do you expect me to believe that?" I ask looking down at her as I swipe at the tears that have escaped, anger and grief twisting together inside me like a blade.

E stands and gently places his hands on my shoulders. His hazel eyes locking onto mine with an intensity that makes it impossible to look away.

"Isabella, listen to me," he says, his voice low and calming. "I know this is a lot to process. I know it's hard not to believe this is your fault. But you have to remember—this is not the end. You and Julian, you have a bond that transcends these realms. This isn't the last time you'll see him. When your life ends, it's not the end of your story. There's so much more. Life on Earth is temporary."

His words slowly sinking in. Little by little, the anger bubbling inside me and the panic wrapping around my chest begin to fade. I don't know what he did or how he did it, but he's managed to soothe the storm raging within me.

I don't know what E did or how, but somehow, he's managed to reach me—pulling me out of the spiral before I can drown in it.

"Okay, I'm sorry," I say, my voice trembling. "It's just … I don't know how to take all this in and still be expected to save the realms."

Julian steps closer, gently taking my hand in his. This time, I don't pull away. I take comfort in the warmth of his touch.

"We don't expect you to take everything in without feeling," E says gently, kindly. "But that's why we are here. To guide you and support you.

I let out a breath. "Thanks," I murmur, then glance between them. "So … what's the plan now?"

CHAPTER 40

The clatter of a pan hitting the floor jolts me awake. My body feels heavy, my mind sluggish—last night's trip to the other realm left me drained and uneasy. We hadn't come up with a solid plan, just the same vague advice to trust my instincts and rely on my bracelet when neither my guardian angels nor Julian can protect me. Not exactly reassuring.

I drag myself out of bed, still weighed down by exhaustion, but I need to check if everything downstairs is okay.

"Buenos días, Elle. I hope I'm not the reason you're awake," Sara says as I step into the kitchen.

I let out a yawn before I can stop it, quickly covering my mouth.

"I'm so sorry, Elle! I was trying to be as quiet as possible, but I'm just all over the place today," she says, pulling a handful of vegetables out of the refrigerator and setting them on the counter.

I narrow my eyes. Sara is usually well put-together, and the only times I've seen her this flustered is when she's nervous about something.

I slide into a chair at the kitchen table, crossing my arms. "A ver, qué o quién es," I say, giving her a knowing look.

She nearly drops the tomato in her hand, her gaze snapping to mine like a kid caught sneaking cookies. "¿De qué hablas?" she asks, letting out a nervous chuckle.

"Come on, Sara. Te conozco," I say, leaning back in my chair, my eyebrow raised.

Sara hesitates. Then she lets out a sigh, abandoning the pretense and takes a seat beside me. Her fingers trace the edge of the table, her expression shifting into something softer.

"I took your advice," she says, finally meeting my gaze. "I cut Joe out of my life."

"¡Qué bueno! You deserve so much better," I say, nodding in approval.

"Yeah ... well," she hesitates, her cheeks turning pink. "I met someone else. They asked me on a date tonight."

A laugh slips out before I can stop it, the sound startling even me. But the way Sara's face flushes deepens, I stop. She looks embarrassed—bashful in a way I haven't seen in years.

"Perdón," I say, holding back a grin. "It's just—you're so cute about it. It's like you're in high school again."

She rolls her eyes at me. "Whatever. Anyway, he's stopping by to introduce himself to you guys. He said he wanted to be respectful."

I raise an eyebrow, impressed. "Wow. That's rare these days. Where'd you find a guy like that?"

"At work, actually. We met in the cafeteria. He's a heart surgeon, and he had just finished a surgery when I bumped into him."

"When did all this happen?" I ask, leaning forward, curiosity piqued.

"It was back in March, shortly after Julian's passing." Her voice trails off, and she looks down at the table, her fingers absently tracing the edge of the table again. "He's been pursuing me for several months now, but I didn't feel ready. I wanted to be here for you, too …"

At the mention of Julian, the mood in the room shifts, the laughter fading into a quiet heaviness. I reach over and give her hand a gentle squeeze, hoping it's enough to show her that I understand.

I can't undo what's happened over the past six months, but maybe I can help us all find a way to start moving forward, despite everything else that's happening.

"Well, what time is he coming over?" I ask, steering the conversation back to the topic of my sister's new man.

"He said 6:00 p.m. Manny's going to be here too—he insisted." She finally looks back at me, her lips curving into the smallest smile.

"Well then," I say with mock seriousness, "I'll make sure I'm on my best behavior. Wouldn't want to scare him off before he even gets through the door."

Her laughter is soft but genuine, and it sparks a small flicker of relief inside me.

By the time 6:00 p.m. rolls around, the house feels alive in a way it hasn't in months. Manny's booming voice carries from the kitchen as he chats with Sara, his laughter spilling into the living room. I sit on the couch, absentmindedly tugging at a loose thread on my sleeve, counting the seconds until I meet my sister's new man.

The doorbell rings, sharp and startling, and Sara practically sprints to answer it. Manny stretches with a grunt before wandering over to sit beside me. "Vamos a ver," he says with a teasing grin, nudging me lightly. I grin back at him, the anticipation growing.

When they step into the living room, we're greeted by a tall man with a smile that reaches his dark eyes. His movements are calm and confident, and he smells faintly of cedar and something crisp, like citrus. Manny stands up and shakes his hand first, firm but not overbearing, then turns to Sara with a gentleness in his expression that catches my attention.

There's something in the way he looks at her, something kind. Maybe this will actually be good for her.

Then he steps closer to me, prompting Manny to shift to Sara's side to give him space.

"Hi, I'm Omar," he says, extending his hand. His voice is smooth, his broad frame towering over me. I stand to shake his hand, suddenly aware of just how imposing his size is. His shoulders block Manny and Sara from view, making me feel uncomfortably small.

The moment our eyes meet, a chill runs down my spine. The air around me feels heavier, the world tilting slightly out of focus. For an instant, his dark eyes flash red—just long enough to make my heart stutter, my breath catching.

His warm smile twists, just for a second, into something else. Something mocking.

"It's only a matter of time, Isabella," he murmurs, his voice low, each word slicing through me like a blade. "You can't escape your fate."

A jolt of fear makes me stumble back. My pulse hammers in my ears. Then, as quickly as it came, the moment is gone.

Omar blinks, his expression as open and friendly as before. Normal. No red eyes, no twisted smile. As if nothing was ever there.

Did I just imagine that?

"Hi, I'm Omar," he says again, his tone warm and polite, as though nothing happened. Manny and Sara remain completely unaware, smiling as though everything is fine.

I stare at him, my hand still hovering awkwardly in the air. My mind races, trying to make sense of what I just saw—or thought I saw. Slowly, I take his hand, my fingers trembling. His grip is light and brief, and then he's already turning his attention back to Manny and Sara, slipping into easy conversation. As though the last few seconds never existed.

They're trying to scare you.

A? I call out in my mind, my thoughts frantic.

"It's working," I think bitterly. *Can they… possess humans? Is Omar one of them?*

"*No, Omar is not an angel of death,*" A's voice responds in my mind. "*Angels of death can momentarily possess humans, but they cannot harm you. Remember, your bracelet is protecting you.*"

I exhale slowly, forcing myself to steady my breathing. My trembling hand instinctively touches the bracelet on my wrist. Reminding me that I'm safe. For now.

After a friendly chat, Omar and Sara leave to go on their date. Manny nudges me on the shoulder.

"Vamos, hermanita," he says with a grin. "Let's go on a date of our own."

I smile up at him. "¡Sale!"

We leave the house and head to one of my favorite sushi restaurants. The familiar scent of soy sauce and fresh fish greets us as we step inside, instantly lifting my mood. I haven't had sushi in so long, and the flavors of a special roll takes me back to simpler, happier times. I eat until I feel like my stomach is about to explode.

"¿Quieres algo más?" Manny asks, glancing over the menu, clearly debating whether or not to get dessert.

"No manches, Manny! Estoy bien llena. How do you still have room for dessert?" I ask, shocked at his bottomless appetite.

Manny chuckles, patting his belly with exaggerated satisfaction. "He estado enflacando mucho," he jokes, making me laugh.

Still smiling, I shake my head. "No, I'm good. You order whatever you want. I'll be back—I need to go to the bathroom."

I stand up and head toward the restrooms, tucked away at the back of the restaurant, far from the lively chatter and warm glow of the dining area. The further I walk, the dimmer the lights become. A light chill runs down my spine, but I brush it off. *It's nothing*

I push open the bathroom door and step inside. The second I do, the lights begin to violently flicker, casting eerie, fleeting shadows across the walls.

I stop dead in my tracks, my heart pounding as my gaze locks onto it. There's a shadowy figure standing perfectly still at the far end of the restroom.

It doesn't move. It doesn't speak. But its presence is overwhelming, filling the room with a suffocating, oppressive energy. My breath hitches in my throat, the invisible weight of its gaze pinning me where I stand.

The figure lingers for a few seconds, unmoving, before vanishing completely. The lights stop flickering as though nothing happened.

My heart pounds in my chest, but my body refuses to move. It feels like I'm glued to the floor, the fear rooting me in place.

The bathroom door creaks open behind me, and I let out a startled yelp.

"Oh, sorry! I didn't mean to scare you," an older woman says with a kind smile before walking past me into one of the stalls.

I force myself to smile back, nodding to signal that everything is fine.

But it's not.

The angels of death are closer than I thought—and they're getting bolder.

A was right. They're trying to scare me. They want me to know they can get to me, no matter what A, E, or Julian have told me.

I can't hide from them forever.

CHAPTER 41

Later that night, I struggle to fall asleep. Or maybe it's not so much the inability to sleep as it is the fear of it. I'm terrified of dreaming—terrified that La Muerte might show up again.

The sound of the front door closing snaps me out of my thoughts. I check my phone—it's 11:55 p.m. Sara must have had a good time. I hear her footsteps climbing the stairs, followed by a soft knock on my door.

Before I can respond, she pops her head in.

"Elle? You asleep?" she whispers.

"No," I whisper back.

I reach over and switch on the lamp. Sara squints against the sudden light, stepping inside and quietly closing the door behind her, careful not to make too much noise and wake Manny.

"I didn't wake you up, did I?" she asks.

"No," I say, sitting up. "I'm just having a hard time falling asleep," I admit.

She frowns, settling at the edge of my bed. "Everything okay?"

"Yeah, just a little restless," I reply, brushing it off. Then I smirk, eager to shift the focus. "But enough about me—the real chisme here is your date. How was it?" I ask, raising an eyebrow as I change the subject.

Sara's face brightens instantly. "It was great," she says, her smile growing. "Being with Omar is so different from when I was with Joe. He's attentive, he listens, and he's definitely not your typical machista Latino man." She grins, the glow on her face making it clear just how much fun she had.

"But I'll give you all the details in the morning," she adds, stifling a yawn. Unsuccessfully.

"Okay, but I expect all the details," I reply with a teasing smile.

I don't know what the future of the world will look like. Whether I'll destroy it or save it, I really don't know. But I appreciate moments like these with my siblings. Moments that feel normal. Moments that make me forget, even if it's for a second, that I hold the fate of the realms in my hand.

Sara nods, flashing me a sleepy smile before slipping out of my room. The door clicks softly shut behind her, and I settle back into bed.

My thoughts drift, and without thinking, I call out to Julian.

I sense him before I see him. A moment later, he's there, standing at the edge of my bed, his figure half-hidden in shadow.

"Couldn't sleep?" he asks, his voice soft, barely above a whisper.

I shake my head, the weight of the day still clinging to me. "Just needed to see you," I murmur, reaching out a hand.

Without hesitation, he takes it, his fingers warm against mine, grounding me in a way that nothing else can.

"Lay with me for a minute?" I ask, patting the empty space beside me.

Julian doesn't hesitate. He climbs into bed, settling beside me as I scoot closer, resting my head against his chest. The absence of a heartbeat beneath my ear is a quiet, aching reminder that he no longer belongs to this world.

He wraps an arm around me, pulling me closer.

For several minutes, neither of us speaks. There's no need to. The silence between us is comforting, heavy with unspoken words and years of shared understanding. I'm sure he knows what happened today, but he also knows I don't want to talk about it.

Right now, all I need is this.

In the soft glow of the lamplight, I catch the faintest trace of a smile on his face—subtle and fleeting, like a secret meant just for me.

He squeezes my hand gently. "Get some rest." he says, his arm tightening around me.

He holds me the way he always used to, his embrace steady and reassuring. I close my eyes, letting his warmth envelop me. With Julian here, everything feels safe—like everything might actually be okay. His slow, even breaths lull me, and before I know it, sleep begins to pull me under.

CHAPTER 42

I wake up to an empty bed, sunlight streaming through the curtains, casting a warm glow across the room. I reach for my phone on the nightstand, the screen lighting up to reveal the time: 8:55 a.m. It's quiet—I must be the first one up since I don't hear anyone moving around downstairs.

I stretch, shaking off the last traces of sleep, and climb out of bed. I'm feeling generous today. Manny and Sara are always up before me, making breakfast while I sleep in. Today, I think I'll do something for them.

I walk into my closet and pick out a pair of shorts, a simple t-shirt, and sneakers, then carry them downstairs. At the door, I slip them on, ready to start the day.

But as I stand here hand hovering over the doorknob, I realize I didn't think this through. I was planning to pick up pan dulce, but our go-to bakery is a ten-minute drive. Too far to walk there and back in time.

For a brief moment, I consider driving.

Then, my chest tightens.

I haven't been behind the wheel since Julian's accident. My car has been sitting untouched in the garage, except for the rare times Manny takes it out to keep it in good condition. I know it's there, waiting.

But I just can't bring myself to drive. Not yet.

I rethink my plan. *I'll just call a car.* I pull out my phone and open my favorite ride-share app, reserving a car that should arrive in three minutes.

When the car pulls up in front of the house, I take a deep breath, step outside, and get in. Now that I think about it, this is the first time I've gone anywhere by myself since everything happened.

By the time I arrive at the bakery, I'm already regretting my decision. The place is packed, filled with people eagerly picking out pan dulce for breakfast. Of course, it's the weekend—what did I expect?.

I weave my way through the crowded bakery, the smell of freshly baked bread filling the air as I begin picking out the pieces I know Manny and Sara love most. It takes me twenty minutes just to escape the chaos and another fifteen to finally get back home.

As I step through the door, I spot Manny walking into the kitchen. His eyes land on the bag in my hands, surprise flickering across his face.

"Did you go buy pan dulce?" he asks, blinking like he can't quite believe it.

"Sí, ¿y?" I shrug, setting the bag on the counter. "Get the coffee ready," I add, motioning toward the coffee maker.

"¿Y ahora también eres mandona?" he teases, a grin spreading across his face as he heads to the coffee maker.

I grin and turn toward the stairs to wake up Sara, but before I reach them, she's already coming down.

"Elle, is it true that you went to get pan?" Sara asks, surprised, as she reaches the bottom of the stairs.

"Yes, I did. It wasn't a big deal," I reply, feigning annoyance.

Manny and Sara exchange a little chuckle, their laughter light and genuine. I'm sure they appreciate these small, ordinary moments as much as I do.

As we finish up breakfast, an idea strikes me. "How about we go to the pool today?" I suggest, looking between them. "We haven't really enjoyed the summer, and it's almost over. Let's soak up what's left of it."

Sara's face lights up instantly. "Yes! Let's go!" she exclaims, already jumping up from the table, excitement sparkling in her eyes.

Manny sighs, shaking his head with a small smile, but I catch the subtle nod of agreement. I know he's not the biggest fan of pools, but he's willing to go along with it— maybe because it's the first time in a long while that I've been the one suggesting a family outing.

Together, we clear the table, load the dishes into the dishwasher, and start gathering our things.

As I walk upstairs to grab my swimsuit, a soothing sense of warmth settles over me. It's a feeling that I hadn't realized I'd been missing.

Today, it's just us. No worries, no heaviness.

Just a simple summer day with my family.

CHAPTER 43

By the time we get back from the pool, we're all exhausted. The day was perfect, enjoying the last days of summer and spending time with my siblings. We each head to our rooms to shower, agreeing to order pizza for dinner.

After my shower, I slip into comfy lounge clothes and head downstairs, my skin still warm from the sun. Manny is already sprawled out on the couch, phone in hand, scrolling through pizza options. He glances up as I walk around the couch, a tired but content smile on his face.

"Pepperoni?" he asks.

"Siempre," I reply, sinking onto the couch beside him.

A few minutes later, Sara joins us, her damp hair falling over her shoulders. She plops down on my other side, pulling a throw blanket over her lap.

"Did you already order the pizza?" she asks, glancing at Manny.

"Yup. One pepperoni and one Hawaiian," he says, now flipping through a list of movie options on his phone.

"Ew! How many times do I have to tell you—pineapple does NOT belong on pizza," Sara groans, grabbing a throw pillow and tossing it at him. It misses, landing with a pathetic thud behind the couch.

I can't help it—I laugh. A real, genuine laugh.

Of all the things to argue about, it's this—pineapple on pizza. Their voices rise and fall in playful debate, neither willing to back down. There's no tension, no weight pressing down on me. Just them, just us. A fleeting, ordinary moment. *God, I've missed this.* I wish life could always be this easy, where the hardest decision I have to make is whose side to take in a never-ending pizza war.

If only for today, I just want to stay in this moment with them, let the rest of my worries fade into the background—even if only for a little while.

The doorbell rings about twenty minutes later, cutting through Manny and Sara's still-heated argument. I shake my head, half-amused, wondering how they managed to stretch such a small topic into a full-blown debate.

Manny gets up to grab the pizza, leaving Sara behind with a smug look, as if she's won by default. I roll my eyes at her, but a smile tugs at my lips.

He returns with the boxes, setting them on the coffee table. As he opens one, the mouthwatering aroma of pepperoni and melted cheese fills the room, making my stomach growl. We each grab a slice, barely bothering with plates.

Manny puts on a movie, but it's mostly just background noise as we eat and listen to Sara gush about Omar and their date. I stay quiet, a small smile on my face, happy just to see her happy.

We nearly finish both pizzas, including the Hawaiian one that Sara and Manny spent so much time arguing over. My body feels heavy, the exhaustion from the day settling deep into my limbs. I can see it in my siblings too. Manny lets out a loud yawn, and Sara soon follows, her eyelids drooping as she sinks into the couch.

"Looks like we could all use some rest," I say.

"Can't argue with that," Sara mumbles, standing up and stretching. She heads for the stairs. "Hasta mañana. Los veo en la mañana."

"Don't forget to set your alarm. We're going to church tomorrow," Manny calls after her.

Sara waves in acknowledgment without turning around, disappearing up the stairs.

I stand too and offer Manny a hand. He takes it, and I help him to his feet. He slings an arm around my shoulders, and I wrap an arm around his waist as we walk toward the stairs together.

"Manny, gracias por todo. Eres el mejor hermano," I say, leaning into him and giving him a small squeeze.

"¿Y tú, qué tienes?" he asks, glancing down at me.

"Nothing," I murmur. "I just love you."

His arm tightens around me briefly. "I love you too."

At the top of the stairs, he gives my shoulder one last squeeze before letting go.

"Buenas noches," he says, his voice low, warm.

"Buenas noches," I reply, watching as he disappears into his room.

I linger for a moment at the top of the stairs, the quiet settling over the house. These little moments with Manny and Sara remind me of everything I'm fighting for. I have to protect the loved ones I still have.

But as I step into my room and close the door behind me, the reality of everything else slowly creeps back in. The angels of death, La Muerte, the looming prophecy. They're still out there, waiting for me. No matter how much I want to hold on to tonight, I know it won't last forever.

My eyes drift to my bracelet. *I'm not alone,* I remind myself.

For now, that's enough.

CHAPTER 44

Sunday passes without incident. No dreams last night either, which feels like a small blessing.

We went to Mass, as we always do, but I couldn't stop questioning everything I thought I knew about faith and religion. So much of what A and E have revealed contradicts what I was taught as a Catholic. Everything feels different now and I don't know what to believe anymore.

Still, I've fallen into the routine of going to Sunday mass with Sara and Manny, and I don't want to break it. I don't want to raise any alarms or make them suspect that something's wrong.

So, I sit beside them in the pews, quietly following along with the prayers, standing and kneeling when expected. But my mind drifts, tangled up in all the contradictions and unanswered questions swirling in my head.

When night falls, I lie in bed, staring at the ceiling I've memorized by now, my thoughts as restless as ever.

Ever since the angel of death appeared before me, I've been trying to ignore the inevitable. But the truth is, I can't keep running. I can't keep hiding behind the protection of my guardian angels and Julian. If I'm going to face them, I need answers.

A and E tell me I'm stronger than I think—that I have what it takes to protect myself. Maybe they're right. Maybe I just need to believe it.

I glance at my phone. The screen lights up, displaying the time. 11:55 p.m.

If I'm going to do this, I need to do it now—before I lose my nerve.

I take a deep breath and settle into my bed, pulling the covers up to my shoulders. My heartbeat echoes in my ears as I close my eyes and exhale slowly.

This has to work.

I focus on my breathing—slow, steady, deliberate. Inhale. Exhale. I let the rhythm carry me away, my body sinking deeper into the mattress as the edges of consciousness begin to blur.

The pull of the dream realm tugs at me, gentle but insistent. That familiar weightlessness sets in, and I feel myself drifting further and further away from the waking world.

When I open my eyes, I'm standing in a dark forest. It's not the exact same one, but it's eerily similar to where I've encountered La Muerte before. The trees rise around me like silent sentinels, their gnarled branches clawing at the starless sky.

The air is heavy, almost suffocating.

And, as before, the place is utterly devoid of noise. No wind. No rustling leaves. Just an oppressive silence that presses in from all sides.

I scan my surroundings, my heart pounding against my ribcage. The forest feels alive in a way that makes my skin crawl, as if something unseen is watching me.

And then I spot it.

A figure moves in the distance, barely visible between the twisted trees. My body reacts before my mind does—I instinctively take a step back, every muscle screaming at me to turn and run.

But I don't.

I force myself to take a deep breath, steadying the fear clawing at my chest. The weight of the bracelet on my wrist reminds me that I'm protected. *You can do this. You have to do this.*

I stand my ground, straightening my posture, and take a step forward. My knees feel weak, but I put on the bravest face I can conjure.

"I'm here," I say, my voice cutting through the silence. It trembles slightly, but I don't back down. "Isn't this what you wanted?"

The leaves rustle in response—soft at first, then louder. The figure steps closer, its silhouette sharpening against the shadows.

It emerges slowly, deliberately, as if savoring my unease. My eyes strain to make sense of it. Its form flickers in and out of focus. It's tall and impossibly thin, with limbs that seem just a little too long, bending in unnatural ways.

My breath catches as its face—or the void where a face should be—tilts toward me.

This isn't the first time I've seen La Muerte. But it's never looked like this before. It's twisting itself into something worse, something meant to unnerve me. It's testing me, trying to see how far I'm willing to take this.

And I'm willing. I have to be. I need answers.

"Gracias por venir, Isabella," La Muerte says, its voice low and chilling, sending an icy shiver down my spine. I clench my fists, forcing myself to mask my reaction and stand tall.

"Entonces, ¿me vas a decir qué es lo que quieres conmigo?" I snap, cutting straight to the point. "I'm tired of all the games."

The figure takes a step closer, and then it begins to shift.

What emerges from the shadows is no longer the skeletal form I've come to associate with La Muerte.

No.

Now, it's a man.

CHAPTER 45

He's tall, easily over six feet, with striking features that seem almost too perfect. His broad shoulders fill out a sharp black suit, perfectly tailored to his muscular frame. His smooth, luminous skin carries warm golden undertones, and his piercing dark eyes—almond-shaped and razor-sharp—lock onto mine with an intensity that sends a chill through my chest.

His high cheekbones and strong jawline give him an elegant, almost regal presence, but it's his long, jet-black hair—loosely tied back with a few strands framing his face—that adds to the deliberate, calculated perfection of his appearance.

Every movement he makes is fluid, deliberate, and unnervingly precise, as though he's spent eons mastering the art of intimidation—and seduction.

For a moment, I falter.

Elle! Don't get distracted! This is what it wants!

I snap myself out of it, shaking my head and forcing my thoughts back into focus.

I clench my jaw. "You expect me to be flattered?"

He chuckles, the sound rich and unhurried. "Not flattered. Just comfortable." His dark eyes gleam with something unreadable.

I scoff. "You act like we're friends. We're not." I take a step forward, refusing to be intimidated. "Why do you want to end the world?"

La Muerte exhales. "Skipping the pleasantries, I see. Straight to the point—just like you, Isabella." He smirks. "But you and your guardian angels have it all wrong."

I narrow my eyes. "What do you mean we got it all wrong?" I demand, my voice sharp. "So you're not trying to end the world to make your own order?"

La Muerte lets out a long, exasperated sigh, dragging his hand through his tied-back hair. A few loose strands escape the tie, tumbling casually across his features. The gesture is so human that it throws me off for a second.

Is he annoyed? Really? Why is *he* annoyed? I should be the one irritated—the nerve of this … thing.

"Isabella, take a seat. This is going to take some time."

As he speaks, the dark forest begins to shift. The shadows retreat, replaced by soft rays of sunlight filtering through the trees. The gnarled branches smooth out, transforming into vibrant green foliage, their trunks strong and full of life.

Then, as if conjured out of thin air, a table and two chairs materialize in the clearing. The polished wood gleams unnaturally in the softened light, an elegant and jarring contrast to the eerie forest I'd just been standing in.

La Muerte moves with effortless grace, settling into one of the chairs as if this were nothing more than a casual meeting between old acquaintances. With a flick of his hand, he motions for me to join him.

I hesitate, watching him carefully. Everything about this feels wrong. *Everything about him feels wrong.* But despite my better judgment, I step forward, pulling out the empty chair across from him and lowering myself into it.

The fear that had gripped me earlier is gone now, replaced by something else—curiosity. It gnaws at me, stubborn and insistent.

La Muerte leans back in his chair, resting an elbow on the armrest as he studies me, as though he's deciding just how much to reveal.

Finally, he speaks, his voice low. "A funny thing happened to me," he says, his tone almost conversational, as if recounting a casual story over coffee. "As I moved between realms, I began to notice… shifts. Subtle at first. Then undeniable. I was changing. Developing free will. And with it came questions—questions no angel of death is ever meant to ask. What. Who. When. Why."

He pauses, his dark eyes holding mine, unblinking, as if daring me to look away.

"I tried speaking to the others—the other angels of death—but they couldn't understand." His voice dips lower, almost thoughtful. "That's when I knew. I had broken free. Slipped the bonds of the blind, unquestioning loyalty that binds us all to God."

My breath catches slightly, but I stay silent, too caught up in his words to interrupt.

"Don't get me wrong," he continues, his tone softening. "I love God. I truly do. And it's because I love God that I'm doing what I'm doing. My mistake wasn't asking questions—it was daring to share them. To bring my ideas to the archangels."

He leans forward now, resting his elbows on the table, his distinct features more striking in the soft, surreal light filtering through the clearing. His intensity is overwhelming, impossible to ignore.

"But they didn't like my ideas," he says, his voice laced with quiet bitterness. "So they did what they always do when something doesn't fit neatly into their perfect order. They banished me. Cast me out of the divine realm. Stripped me of my place among the heavenly ranks.

I stay silent, unsure how to respond, and he presses on.

"But what they didn't realize," he says, his voice gaining an edge, "was that banishment didn't sever my connection to the other angels of death. It only freed me. It gave me the space to wake them up. To show them the truth. And together, we started … researching."

"Researching?" I ask, fidgeting in my seat as unease prickles at my skin.

"Yes." He leans forward slightly, his sharp eyes narrowing. "You see, Isabella, you're the reincarnation of the previous Realm Destroyer—or the Beacon of Hope, depending on who you ask. But that truth was deliberately buried by God. Erased. Forgotten." His voice drops lower. "God believed that by wiping out every record, every memory tied to that identity, it could protect you from me."

I blink, struggling to keep up with his words. "God can erase memories? And what happened to the previous person?" My voice feels small, my thoughts spinning.

"Yes, God can erase memories. God can do anything— though it tends to act subtly, without overstepping." He gives me a faint, mocking smile. "After all, God works in mysterious ways."

His expression darkens. "As for the previous Realm Destroyer …" He pauses. "She sacrificed herself to save all the realms. A noble act, really. She ensured she couldn't be used, and for that, God erased all records of the prophecy, so no one could exploit the next Realm Destroyer."

Realm Destroyer. He keeps saying that, and I don't like it. It's as if he's already decided that I'll destroy all the realms, that I'll play right into his hands. The thought makes my skin crawl. I'm not his pawn, and I don't like the way he speaks about me, as though my fate has already been sealed.

La Muerte smirks, tilting his head. "What, don't like the nickname?"

I narrow my eyes at him, glaring silently—it's the only response I can manage. My defiance only seems to amuse him, and he lets out a low, mocking laugh.

Then a thought strikes me, and I lean forward, giving him a mocking smile of my own. "How are you any different from Lucifer?" I ask, my tone sharp and taunting, hoping to strike a nerve.

It works. His smirk vanishes, replaced by a dark snarl. "Don't you dare compare me to that fallen angel," he snaps, his voice cold and laced with venom.

I don't back down. If anything, I push further, my smile unwavering. "But don't you both share the same goal? You both believe humans are corrupted. You're both trying to prove it to God, aren't you?" I press, deliberately pushing his buttons.

"Lucifer and I do not share the same goals or mindset," he says, his voice dripping with venom. "Lucifer was driven by pride, envy, and greed. He thought he was better than God, that he deserved to be worshipped. He wanted everything for himself. That is not love for God."

"But he also started a rebellion," I press, my tone sharper now. "Isn't that exactly what you're doing?"

His hands slam down on the table, the force reverberating through the air.

I flinch.

He rises to his full height, leaning forward until his face is just inches from mine. The sudden intensity of his movements makes me instinctively shrink back, the heat of his fury rolling off him in waves.

I stare at him, too afraid to look away.

When he speaks again, his voice is low.

"Humans alone will never be able to free themselves from their own sins," he says, his tone hard, unyielding. "They are easily tempted, too entangled in the world's corruption. For that, they will never reach the doors of Heaven. Humanity has lost its way. I want to create a world where they are finally free of sin, where they can experience the boundless love of God."

He leans even closer, his piercing eyes locking onto mine.

"And in order for that to happen, Isabella, I need you to help me destroy this corrupted realm—and the rest."

He pauses, letting the words hang in the air. Goosebumps rising across my skin.

I shrink back slightly, but his voice changes, growing almost soothing.

"I don't want to harm you, Isabella. That's where you're all wrong."

I hold my breath, waiting, as he continues.

"I need you alive and well. The gift God gave you—it allows you to open portals between realms. Once you master it, you'll be unstoppable. You could bring beings across realms—or banish them entirely. Think of what you could do!"

He watches me closely, trying to assess my reaction. Then, calmly, he adds, "It's been a rough start, I admit, but I needed you to grow into your gift. You're not grasping it as quickly as the previous Realm Destroyer, but you're getting there. Slowly, yes—but surely."

He leans in slightly, his voice lowering. "You don't need your guardian angels to teach you. You already know how to use it. You just have to trust yourself. But you've been too afraid to let the power course through you. Deep down you've always known you had this power. You've just been afraid to accept what you are."

His words chill me to my core. My chest tightens, and for a moment, I can't breathe.

Something about what he said wakes something inside me that I don't like.

I don't want to be here anymore.

I just want to go home.

I want to see Julian.

Panic starts to build, coiling tight in my stomach. Each breath feels harder to pull in than the last, and my heart pounds like it's trying to break free from my chest. I need to leave—away from him, away from this twisted place.

I shake my head firmly. "I don't trust you," I manage to say, though my voice trembles.

La Muerte reaches toward me, his expression calm but unnerving, his hand outstretched. "You will, Isabella. In time—Isabella don't!"

Before his hand can reach me, I jolt awake, gasping for air as though I've just surfaced from drowning.

"Chave!"

Julian's voice cuts through the haze of my panic, and I turn to see him rushing toward me from the corner of the room.

I don't wait. I stumble out of bed, crashing into his chest, my arms wrapping around him as tightly as I can. I press my face against him, shaking, desperately needing his warmth, his strength, him.

CHAPTER 46

It took Julian half an hour to calm me down before I could bring myself to tell him what I'd done. He wasn't happy—his furrowed brow and clenched jaw said as much. But he didn't leave. He stayed. He stayed with me, holding me until I finally drifted back to sleep.

This time, there were no dreams. Just darkness.

But now that I'm awake, the weight of everything settles over me like a heavy blanket. There's so much to process, so much that doesn't make sense.

We had it all wrong.

A and E believed that La Muerte wanted to bring an end to the world for selfish reasons. But that's not what La Muerte wants.

I don't know what's true anymore.

Was it all just a manipulation? A way to get me on its side?

"Ugh!" I groan, running my hands through my hair in frustration as I pace my room. My thoughts churn in endless circles, pulling me deeper into a spiral.

Six months ago, I was just a grieving widow, struggling to survive in a world that felt hollow without Julian. I didn't have "gifts" or prophecies hanging over me. I was normal. Just trying to figure out how to live without my person.

How did all of that change? *When* did all of that change?

I stop pacing and sink onto the bed, dropping my head into my hands.

I don't want this. I don't want any of this. I just want to go back to my normal life. Even if it means not being able to see Julian again.

The thought makes my chest ache, a hollow ache, deep and consuming. But it's true. This is too much. All of this is too much.

The doorbell rings, breaking through my spiraling thoughts. I freeze, instinctively waiting for Manny or Sara to answer it—until I remember it's a weekday. They're both at work.

The doorbell rings again, sharper this time.

I sigh, forcing myself to my feet, and head downstairs. My mind races with possibilities as I reach the door.

"Ximena?" I ask, startled to see one of my sisters-in-law standing there. Her presence here is the last thing I expected.

"Hi, Isabella," she says, her voice awkward, hesitant, like someone trying to navigate uncharted territory.

She stands on the porch, hands clasped in front of her, her gaze darting to the ground as if searching for the right words.

It takes me a few seconds to process her presence before my manners kick in.

"Come in," I say, stepping back to make room for her to enter. "Sorry, I just wasn't expecting you to be the one knocking at my door." My voice is polite, but there's an edge to it I can't quite hide.

Ximena offers a tight-lipped smile and steps past me, her movements hesitant, as if she's unsure whether she truly belongs here.

We walk to the living room in silence, the air between us thick with unspoken words and the weight of old wounds. I gesture toward the sofa, inviting her to sit, while I settle onto the loveseat beside her.

The familiar comfort of the room feels distant now, replaced by the tension that swirls between us.

Ximena sits carefully, her eyes flitting around the room, taking in the space that Julian and I once shared. Her discomfort is obvious. She looks like she's searching for something—maybe the right words to start, or perhaps the courage to follow through.

"Thank you for receiving me," Ximena says finally, her voice quiet, tentative. "I honestly didn't think you would—not after how things ended the last time I saw you."

She pauses, clasping her hands in her lap, her knuckles whitening as she wrestles with her thoughts.

"I've been meaning to apologize since that day," she continues, her words halting, as if every word costs her something. "For my mom, for not saying anything …

for not defending you when I should have. I just—I just couldn't find the courage to reach out. We've all been processing Julian's passing in our own ways, which I know isn't an excuse. But still ... I'm sorry."

Her apology hangs in the air, heavy and unresolved. I can feel her eyes on me, watching closely, searching for something—an opening, a sign of forgiveness, anything.

But I'm not sure what my face is giving her right now. Anger? Sadness? Anxiety? Relief?

A storm of emotions churns inside me, each one fighting to take over, leaving me unable to find solid ground. For so long, I thought about what I'd say if Ximena ever came back into my life. Now she's here, and all I feel is chaos.

I don't accept the apology right away. I know that's not the real reason she's here.

"Okay," I say, my voice even but guarded. "So, what brings you here?"

Ximena shifts uncomfortably in her seat, her lips pressing together as though weighing her words carefully. After a long pause, she takes a deep breath, as if trying to gather courage.

"My mom fell ill a few weeks ago," she says, her voice quiet. "She's been struggling. Julian's passing hit her the hardest."

Anger bubbles within me, sharp and relentless, cutting through the whirlwind of other emotions swirling around.

Of course your mother took Julian's passing hard. But what about me? How do you think it's been for me?

None of you even know that I tried to take my own life because the thought of living in a world without him was unbearable. But how could you know?

None of you ever cared enough to ask how I was doing, not once. You didn't check in, didn't reach out—not before, not after. Even during my marriage, your family never truly accepted me. Julian was the only connection I had to any of you.

And now he's gone.

But I don't say any of that. I push the words down, swallowing the bitterness threatening to spill over.

Instead, I reply, "And what does that have to do with me?"

My voice comes out colder than I intend, sharp enough to slice through the fragile thread of civility holding this conversation together. But Ximena being here—after all this time—is stirring up emotions I thought I had buried.

Ximena flinches at my tone, her discomfort palpable. She hesitates, visibly struggling with the weight of what she's about to say. Her fingers twist together nervously in her lap.

"My mom's treatment has become very expensive. She'll need surgery—it's a matter of life or death. Even with all of us pitching in, we don't have the funds. And we know Julian left you … everything." She glances up at me. "I was wondering if you could spare some of that money to help pay for her surgery."

For a moment, I'm too stunned to react. Then, heat rushes to my cheeks, and my heart pounds with a mix of anger and disbelief.

After everything her mother said to me, after blaming me for taking her son from her, Ximena has the nerve to come into my home and ask me for money to save the life of the woman who vowed never to forgive me?

I stare at Ximena, my mind racing, unsure of what to say.

"So, you weren't really here to apologize?" I begin, my voice tight, trembling with barely suppressed emotion. "Of course not. Because if you were genuine, you would have apologized months ago. If you were genuine, you would have asked me how I was doing. And why is it only you here? Why can't your mom apologize herself?"

My words pour out in a cutting, unrelenting stream, each syllable slicing deeper. I can't seem to stop myself, the dam holding back months of hurt and anger finally breaking.

Ximena's eyes widen, her face frozen in shock. She wasn't expecting this—she thought she could come here and say her piece, and I'd just fall in line. But I can't bring myself to care. There's too much pain, too much anger, and it's all boiling to the surface now, like a wound I can no longer ignore.

"Did any of you know that Julian and I were trying to start a family? Did you know we actually succeeded—but I miscarried at the end of my first trimester? That I had to be admitted to the hospital because of complications?" My voice rises with each word, raw and unfiltered, every syllable heavier than the last. I lean forward, teetering on the edge of my seat, my hands trembling. "Did you know that happened just three months before Julian passed away?"

I can't stop now. The words claw their way out of me, flooding the room with truths I've held in for far too long.

"And the only reason Julian was out the night your mother accused me of killing her son was because I was having a depressive episode. He was trying to comfort me—he wanted to make me feel better, so he went to get my favorite dinner dish and my favorite Mexican treat. And do you know what day it was? The three-month anniversary of losing our baby!"

My voice cracks at the end, but I don't hold back. The weight of those memories, those unspoken moments, presses down on me, and I let it all spill out. The silence in the room feels deafening, like the air has been sucked away.

"Not even Manny or Sara knew," I add, my voice quieter now, trembling with emotion. "We wanted to make it through the first trimester before sharing the news. Julian and I were so excited … And then everything fell apart."

I take a shaky breath, my chest tight, and press forward, unable to stop now.

"There's so much you all don't know—because you never cared to include me as part of your family. Or maybe you were just too scared to go against your mother. Either way, it doesn't matter now. I've gone through so much this year, Ximena. So for your mother to tell me I'll never understand what it feels like to lose a child?"

My voice hardens, and the anger rises again, steadying me, giving me strength. "She was wrong. I understand more than she ever will. And on top of that, I lost the love of my life just a few months later. I will never have the opportunity to start a family with Julian. Never."

The words loom in the air around us, suffocating and final.

Ximena's face pales, her expression frozen in shock. I see the guilt and regret flickering in her wide eyes, but I can't bring myself to look at her anymore. I don't have the energy—not after everything I've just said.

The floodgates have opened, and the flood of emotions is unstoppable now.

Without a word, I stand up and walk to the entryway and motion to the door letting Ximena know that our conversation is over.

Ximena hesitates before stepping past me, her movements uncertain. She pauses at the door, glancing back, her voice barely a whisper. "I'm sorry, Isabella. For everything."

And then she's gone.

The door clicks shut behind her, and the silence that follows is deafening. I collapse to the ground in the entryway, gripping my shirt over my heart as if holding it will somehow stop it from breaking any further—if that's even possible.

Sobs wrack my body, violent and uncontrollable, tears streaming down my face in endless streams. Every emotion I've been fighting to contain—grief, anger, despair—comes rushing to the surface like a tidal wave, crashing over me with relentless force.

A guttural scream tears from my throat, raw and desperate, as if trying to purge all the pain and rage I've been suppressing. It echoes through the empty house.

I scream again, louder this time, taking advantage of the solitude, knowing no one is here to witness me fall apart.

When the energy finally leaves me, all I can do is curl into myself and sob. The tears flow freely, washing over me in an unrelenting storm of anguish. I stay there on the floor, broken, as the weight of everything crushes me into silence.

CHAPTER 47

I don't know how long I stay like that, but eventually, the sobs fade into quiet sniffles, leaving only emptiness. My body feels heavy, too drained to do anything but exist in this moment.

And then I feel it—a warm hand on my shoulder. The touch is gentle but firm, so sudden it makes me flinch. My breath catches as I snap my head up, startled, my tear-streaked face meeting the eyes of the person crouching in front of me.

"Amor," Julian whispers, his voice tender, filled with sadness. His dark eyes, so familiar, mirror the grief I feel in my own chest.

Without thinking, I throw myself into his arms, clutching him as if letting go would make him disappear. The sobs return, spilling out of me as I bury my face in his chest. His embrace is warm.

I know this isn't healthy. I know it's not helping me heal. But right now, none of that matters. All I want—all I need—is to be held in his arms, to feel the illusion of safety his presence brings, and never leave.

Julian doesn't say a word. He just holds me, his arms strong and sure, letting me cry until the tears start to run dry and the sobs fade into soft, uneven sniffles.

When I've finally calmed, I pull back just enough to look at him. His hands move to my face, wiping the tears from my cheeks with a tenderness that breaks me all over again. His thumbs trace gentle circles on my skin. I can see the sadness still lingering in his eyes.

"Julian," I whisper, my voice trembling and small, "I can't do this anymore.

His brows knit together in concern. "Amor…"

I don't let him finish.

The words spill out, broken and raw, before I can stop them. "I can't do this anymore! It's too much!" My voice cracks, rising with the weight of everything I've been holding inside. "I know they say God doesn't give us trials we can't handle, but this—this feels like it's meant to break me. To knock me down and keep me there. How much more am I supposed to endure? How much more am I supposed to overcome?"

My chest heaves as the words pour out of me, raw and unfiltered, and I clutch Julian's shirt like it's the only thing keeping me upright. I can feel the weight of my pain pressing down on every part of me, threatening to suffocate me entirely.

Tears blur my vision, spilling over as I continue, my voice trembling.

"I lost my parents during a time I needed them most, I lost our baby, and I lost *you!* How much more, Julian? How much more am I supposed to endure? And now, with everything else—the angels, La Muerte, the prophecy—I feel like I'm drowning, Julian. I don't know how to keep going. I don't even know if I can keep going."

Julian watches me, his expression pained, but he doesn't speak. His silence feels heavy, like it's holding all the words he can't bring himself to say. I can see his heartbreak reflecting mine, and it only makes my chest ache more.

"It hurts too much to have you like this," I continue, my voice faltering as the emotions threaten to choke me. "To have you here, but not really here. To feel you, to see you, but know we can never share the same life." My throat tightens, and I can barely force the words out. "I'm sorry, Julian, but I need to do this for me. I've never been selfish, but … maybe I need to be."

Julian's lips part, his expression shifting as if he's about to plead with me, but I don't give him the chance. The decision has already been made.

I close my eyes. I don't know how I know, but I do.

Somewhere deep within me, beyond logic or explanation, I understand how to close my third eye. Despite what A and E said, the knowledge isn't something that can be taught. It's something innate, instinctive, undeniable.

La Muerte was right. My gift will come to me naturally. And this?

This feels natural.

I feel the energy building, shifting, gathering inside me like a tidal current waiting for release. My hands tremble as I focus inward, guiding it, shaping it. I know what this will mean—what it will take from me, what it will take from us.

But I also know I have to do it.

"No," Julian whispers, his voice faint now, tinged with desperation. "Please, Chave. Don't ..."

But it's already too late.

I feel the connection sever, like a thread snapping in the wind. Julian's form begins to fade, his edges softening until he's no longer substantial. His image flickers, his features dissolving into nothingness, and then he's gone. The warmth of his presence vanishes with him, leaving me alone in the cold, empty house.

The silence presses down on me, deafening.

Sobs erupt from my chest, raw and unrelenting, shaking my entire body as I collapse to the floor. The pain is overwhelming, clawing at me from the inside out. I grieve for everything—everything I've lost.

For my parents.

For our baby.

For Julian.

And for the life we were supposed to have together, the one I'll never get back.

JULIAN

"She closed her third eye," I say, my voice heavy as I stare at A and E sitting at the table where we usually hold our meetings.

A's brows furrow, her expression immediately tense. "Are you sure?"

"Yes," I reply, sinking into the chair across from them. My hands clench into fists on the table, frustration and sorrow threatening to boil over. "I felt it happen. I saw her do it."

E exhales sharply, leaning back in his chair, his hand rubbing the bridge of his nose. "This complicates everything. Without her third eye open, her connection to the spiritual realm is severed."

"I know that," I snap, my voice harsher than I intend. "You don't think I've thought about what this means? She's shut herself off from me … from us … from *everything*. She's trying to protect herself, but she has no idea what she's actually done. I told you guys from the very beginning that she needed to know everything. But you insisted on keeping her in the dark, and now she's played right into La Muerte's hands."

A flinches slightly at my words—something she rarely does—but she doesn't argue. Her gaze looks past me as if searching for the right words and finding none.

E, however, doesn't take the criticism lightly. "Watch your tone, Julian," he says his voice laced with a warning. "That decision was made to protect her, and you agreed to it back then."

"I agreed because I trusted you," I fire back, standing abruptly, the chair scraping against the floor. "I thought you had her best interests at heart. But this? This is a disaster. Do you realize how much more vulnerable she is now? How much easier it'll be for La Muerte to manipulate her?"

"We *do* realize it," A says quietly, her calm tone doing little to soothe the frustration boiling inside me. "But blaming each other won't help her now."

I run a hand through my hair, pacing the room in an attempt to keep myself from shouting. "She's terrified," I say, my voice softer but no less strained. "She thinks she's protecting herself, but all she's done is isolate herself from the very things that could save her. She has no idea how much danger she's in."

E leans forward, resting his elbows on the table, his expression dark. "She'll have to reopen it eventually. If she doesn't …" He trails off, his jaw tightening, and I know exactly what he's leaving unsaid.

"If she doesn't," I say, finishing the thought for him, "then La Muerte wins. And no one will be able to stop it."

The words hang in the air, heavy with unspoken tension.

A finally breaks the silence. "She may have shut her third eye, but she won't be able to keep it shut forever. As long as her loved ones are in her life, they'll give her a reason to stand her ground—to protect them. It's not going to be easy for La Muerte. She's more resilient than you give her credit for."

I stop pacing and turn to face her, my tone sharp. "I think I know my wife better than anybody."

E stands up abruptly, his chair scraping loudly against the floor. His eyes lock onto mine. "That's enough, Julian. Your love for Isabella is clouding your judgment. You're so focused on protecting her that you're ignoring the bigger picture."

The tension crackles between us like a live wire, his words cutting through the air with the weight of truth I don't want to acknowledge.

He's right, though. My judgment hasn't been the best—not since I've been able to hold Chave in my arms again. Seeing her, feeling her, it's made it harder to think clearly, harder to separate my emotions from what needs to be done.

I let out a heavy sigh, running a hand through my hair. "So what now?"

The question lingers, unanswered. Outside, I sense it—the delicate balance between realms tilting ever so slightly, like a distant tremor stirring in the shadows, waiting to erupt. None of us say it out aloud. But whatever comes next will define everything.

ACKNOWLEDGMENTS

I feel incredibly grateful to be writing these words, knowing that this journey—once just a dream—has finally become a reality. This book wouldn't exist without the love and support of the people who have been in my corner from the very beginning.

To my sister, Lupe Gutierrez, and my husband, Eddie Campos—my very first supporters. You believed in me long before I believed in myself. Your unwavering encouragement, love, and faith gave me the courage to keep moving forward, even when the road felt uncertain.

To my dear friend, Ami Meite Nagel, one of my biggest cheerleaders—thank you for always reminding me that anything is possible. Your friendship means the world to me.

To Transcendent Publishing, especially Shanda Trofe, thank you for turning what once felt like an impossible dream into reality. I'm so grateful for your guidance, patience, and expertise that made this journey possible.

And to my mom and dad, who left everything behind in Mexico to give my siblings and me a better future— this is because of you. Your sacrifices, your hard work, and your resilience gave me the privilege to dream big. Everything I do is a testament to your love, your hard work, and your endless devotion.

To everyone who has supported me along the way— thank you. I couldn't have done this without you.

I am forever grateful.

ABOUT THE AUTHOR

Ana Gutierrez spends most of her time lost in fictional worlds—reading, writing, daydreaming, or binge-watching K-dramas. When she's not playing out a dramatic scene in her head, you'll find her devouring crime or supernatural shows and podcasts, convincing herself she'd make an excellent detective (or at least a great sidekick).

Ana, a proud homebody with a travel bug, believes the best stories are written on a comfy couch but inspired by faraway places.

When Darkness Falls is her debut work. She's already plotting her next adventure—either on the page or in the skies.